"You had a life before we arrived."

"Yes—a lonely, empty life with nothing in it but work. I like having you here, Liv. Believe me."

"You are sweet to us."

He made a disgusted noise, and she smiled sadly. "You are. Don't be macho and funny about it. You've been really kind, Ben, and it's not right to take advantage anymore."

"You're not taking advantage."

"Yes, we are."

"No. Okay, I'll admit as a housekeeper you aren't able to give it your best shot because of the kids, but there are other ways in which you more than earn your keep. Just having someone to come home to—someone who knows me, who can understand my sense of humor, knows my likes and dislikes. Someone who smiles and says, 'How was your day?' when I come in."

"That's not a housekeeper, Ben—that's a wife," she said wistfully.

He looked up, his eyes unreadable. "So marry me."

What happens when you suddenly discover your happy twosome is about to be turned into a...*family*?

Do you panic?
Do you laugh?
Do you cry?
Or...do you get married?

The answer is all of the above—and plenty more!

Share the laughter and the tears as these unsuspecting couples are plunged into parenthood! Whether it's a baby on the way, or the creation of a brand-new instant family, these men and women have no choice but to be

READY FOR BABY

When parenthood takes you by surprise!

**Look out in April 2001 for
TEMPORARY FATHER
by Barbara McMahon**

DELIVERED:
ONE FAMILY
Caroline Anderson

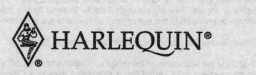

TORONTO • NEW YORK • LONDON
AMSTERDAM • PARIS • SYDNEY • HAMBURG
STOCKHOLM • ATHENS • TOKYO • MILAN • MADRID
PRAGUE • WARSAW • BUDAPEST • AUCKLAND

RECYCLED PAPER

ISBN 0-373-03641-8

DELIVERED:ONE FAMILY

First North American Publication 2001.

CHAPTER ONE

IT WAS a big front door. Big and solid and made of oak, a sturdy door that Liv leant on for a moment while she conjured up the courage to ring the bell.

It was four in the morning, and she was probably the last person Ben wanted to see, but she wasn't in a position to be considerate—not then, with all that had happened. She'd apologise later—if he was still speaking to her! There was no guarantee he would be.

The doorbell echoed eerily through the silent house, and Liv pulled her coat round her and shivered. She wasn't sure if it was cold or shock. Probably both. All she knew was that Ben had to come to the door. He had to be at home—there was nowhere else for her to go.

Because, with this last reckless and impulsive act, Olivia Kensington had come to the end of the line.

'All right, all right,' Ben muttered. 'Hang on, I'm coming.' He ran downstairs, belting his dressing gown securely and flicking on the lights as he reached the darkened hallway.

He turned the key, yanked the door open and blinked as his eyes adjusted to the light.

'Liv?'

She looked up at him, her eyes indistinct, shimmering pools of green and gold in the too bright light of the porch. Her dark hair was artfully rumpled, and her smile was as bright as the light. She was clearly

5

oblivious of the hour and the fact that he had been fast asleep, and Ben was tempted to strangle her.

He was always tempted to strangle her. Instead he propped himself against the door jamb and folded his arms across his chest with a resigned sigh. 'What on earth are you doing here at this time of night?' he asked with the last shred of his usually endless patience. 'You aren't locked out, you're too far from home—so what is it, Liv? Staying with someone locally and the party ended too soon? You got bored? You're lost?'

She shook her head.

'No? OK, I give up. To what do I owe the singular honour of your company at—' he checked his watch '—stupid o'clock in the morning?'

The smile widened, became wry. 'Sorry, it is a bit late. It's just—you know you rang me a few weeks ago to ask if I knew anyone who was looking for a housekeeper's job?'

'Housekeeper?' He went still, anticipating trouble and knowing he wouldn't be disappointed. Not with Liv. 'Yes?' he said cautiously, trying to see into the taxi behind her. Had she dragged some prospective candidate along? At whatever time it was? Only Liv—

'I'd like to apply—if it's still free.'

'You?' For a moment he didn't move, and then he shrugged himself away from the frame and peered down at her more closely. That was when he noticed the smudge of mascara round her eyes, the brittleness of the smile, the slight tremor running through her frame.

'For God's sake, Liv, what's happened?' he said

softly, stepping down into the porch and putting an arm round her.

She dragged in a huge breath and smiled gamely up at him, lifting her shoulders in a devil-may-care shrug, but the smile shattered and her mouth firmed into a grim line. 'He threw me out—Oscar. He said— you don't want to know what he said.' She shuddered. 'Anyway, he threw us out of the door and slammed it—I tried to ring you but my mobile phone doesn't work any more. The bastard must have had it disconnected instantly—he's probably reported it stolen.'

The bitterness and shock in her voice brought a murderous rage boiling to the surface in Ben. He looked past her again to the taxi sitting on his drive with its engine running. The driver cut the engine, and in the silence he could hear the insistent wailing of a tiny baby.

'You've got the children?'

She nodded, and he raked his hands through his close-cropped hair and released a sigh of relief. 'Come in, Liv—all of you, come in,' he said gently.

Her shoulders straightened, pride yanking her upright. 'Ben, I wonder if I could ask a favour? I can't pay the taxi—I cleared out my handbag this morning and I must have forgotten to put my credit card folder back in, and I don't have any cash—' She broke off, biting her lip, and Ben guessed she was at the end of her tether.

'Sure. I'll deal with it. Come in before you freeze.' With a deep sigh he led her inside, sat her down before she fell and went out to the taxi driver.

'What do I owe you?' he asked, and winced at the reply. 'OK. I'll just take the children inside. Could you bring the luggage?'

'No luggage, mate,' the taxi driver told him. 'Just her and the screaming kids. One of them's got a real fruity nappy, as well. Don't envy whoever changes that one!' He chuckled, and Ben opened the back door and reached in, lifting the tiny squalling baby off the broad seat and tucking it carefully into his arms. Poor little beast, he was only about four weeks old—maybe less. Ben couldn't remember exactly.

A toddler with Liv's tumbling dark curls was slumped in the corner, thumb hanging from her lip, fast asleep. The aroma seemed to be coming from her. He carried the baby in to Liv, handed it to her, found the money for the taxi in his wallet and went back for the other child.

She woke, stared at him for a second then started to cry.

'Come on, sweetheart. Mummy's inside,' he reassured her, and held out his hand. She wouldn't trust him that far, but she squirmed off the seat and stumbled to the door. He helped her out of the cab and watched it peel away, stripping his gravel in a way that made him wince.

Oh, well. The little girl was heading determinedly for the front door, leaving a trail of nappy-flavoured fog behind her. Ben followed, shutting the front door and leaning on it, looking down at Liv, seeing her clearly for the first time.

She was exhausted. There were bags under her eyes that were weeks old, her face was drawn, her eyes were bleak and hopeless now she'd stopped pretending, and the despair in them made him want to kill Oscar.

Slowly.

Inch by despicable inch.

He crouched down beside Liv and squeezed her leg. 'Your daughter needs a new nappy.'

She found a smile from somewhere, and his heart turned over. 'I know. I noticed. I don't have one.'

The baby started to cry again, and Ben looked at it thoughtfully.

'Can I help you give him a bottle? Or are you breastfeeding?'

She looked suddenly even sadder, if that were possible. 'I was—Oscar didn't like it. He was jealous. He said it didn't do my figure any good, but I didn't think that was why we'd had children—' She broke off, biting her lip, then looked up at him with eyes that tore his heart. 'Ben, I don't have anything—not for any of us. No bottles, no nappies—nothing. I'm sorry to land on you like this, but I didn't know where else to go—'

She broke off again, hanging on to her control by a thread, and Ben squeezed her knee again and stood up. 'I'll find you some little towels you can use as nappies as a stop-gap, and you can help yourself to anything you need in the kitchen while I go to the shops. There's an all-night supermarket—I can pick up some emergency supplies.'

He ran upstairs, threw on his clothes and ran down again, a handful of little towels at the ready. She was still sitting there without moving, the screaming baby nuzzling at her jumper and the toddler lying against her leg, whining with exhaustion.

'Come on,' he said gently, and helped Liv up and led her through to the kitchen. Then he passed her the towels, took the crying baby and left her to make the best she could of the new makeshift nappies. She took the little girl out to the cloakroom, following his directions, and he could hear them talking in the lulls between the baby's screams.

'Poor little tyke,' he murmured, rocking it gently. 'Do you have a name? Probably something stupid like Hannibal, knowing Oscar.'

'He's called Christopher, after my father. Oscar wasn't interested in his name. I call him Kit for short.'

Ben looked up at her, holding her daughter in her arms, and wondered what else Oscar hadn't been interested in. He hadn't even cared enough to give this brave and lovely girl his name.

'Does he always cry like this?' he asked as Kit struck up again.

'Only when he's hungry, but I haven't got anything to feed him—'

'When did you stop feeding him yourself?' he asked.

'Last week. Why?'

'Because you could try. He might not get much food, but he'd get comfort, surely? Just until I can get to the shops? The supermarket down the road is open twenty-four hours. I can be back in half an hour with some formula and bottles.'

She looked doubtful. 'I could try, but I don't think it'll work. I don't know what else to do, but he's so hungry, I can't bear it.' Tears in her eyes, Liv took him, cradling him tenderly against her shoulder and patting him consolingly, but he didn't want to be consoled. He wanted to be fed, and he was going to scream until it happened.

'I'll put the kettle on for you. Why don't you curl up on those big chairs by the window and settle them down, and I'll nip out? Is there anything you particularly want?'

'The contents of their nursery?' she said drily, with a brave attempt at humour.

'I'll take my mobile phone. The number's here, on the wall. Ring me as you think of things. I'll be back as soon as I can.'

He went through to his garage, pressed the remote to open the door and then the gate, and drove up the road towards the supermarket, deep in thought. So Oscar, the scumbag, had thrown them out empty-handed in the middle of the night, had he? On what feeble pretext?

He wasn't sure he wanted to know. He pulled up at the supermarket, went in and stood staring dumbly at the endless rows of disposable nappies. Some for boys, some for girls, all different sizes and ages, umpteen different makes, with resealable tabs and pretty pictures and a bewildering array of specialist features, each purporting to outdo the other brands.

The formula milk was no better. He stared hopelessly at the different makes and wondered if the wrong one would upset Kit. And what about the girl, Melissa? He couldn't remember her nickname—Maisie or something. What did she eat?

It was a minefield—and his chances of getting through it without being blown apart were so slight it wasn't worth considering. Pulling his mobile phone out of his pocket, he punched in his home number and waited.

The phone startled Liv, waking her and Missy who started to whinge again. Kit was asleep at her breast, too exhausted to cry any more. Without moving him she struggled to her feet and picked the phone up cautiously. 'Hello?'

'What size and brand of nappies and milk formula?' Ben asked without preamble.

She told him, and she could hear him muttering to himself as he went up and down the aisle. 'Got them. How many?'

'Whatever,' she said. 'One packet of each for now. I'll have to sort something out.' She paused for a moment, then abandoned diplomacy, because there was no diplomatic way to ask it, and said, 'I take it you were alone last night? I mean, nobody's about to come downstairs and ask awkward questions or get embarrassed? I didn't mess up a hot date or anything, did I?'

He laughed. Well, she thought it was a laugh. It sounded a little stressed, but it was about five in the morning and he probably was a little stressed. 'No,' he said. 'No hot date. Just my beauty sleep.'

'Ben, I'm sorry,' she said softly, and he stopped laughing.

'Liv, it's OK,' he promised, and she believed him.

'Thanks. Don't forget sterilising stuff for the bottles.'

He muttered something, then cut the connection. Would he manage? It was silly, really, she should have gone with him, but she was so tired, so terribly weary and shocked and disillusioned.

Oddly, she wasn't hurt. Not deeply hurt, the way she should have been. Not gutted. Just wounded pride more than anything, with the cruel things Oscar had said. And angry. Dear God, was she angry! She started to pace round the kitchen, her fury building, and by the time Ben got back she was ready to kill.

He took one look at her, raised an eyebrow and

unpacked the shopping on to the big island unit. 'Formula. Bottles. Sterilising stuff. Food for Maisie.'

'Missy,' she corrected, and the corner of his mouth tipped.

'Missy,' he agreed. 'Nappies—for little boys and big girls. Pyjamas. A dress. Tights. Vests. A sleepsuit for Kit. And—' he put his hand into the bag and pulled it out '—toffees.'

'I love you,' she said earnestly, and grabbed the bag, ripping it open and peeling one. Bliss. How had he remembered?

'Right, Missy,' she said, her teeth firmly stuck together, 'let's get you ready for bed.' She scooped up the armful of baby clothes and then, suddenly aware yet again of the enormity of their imposition, she looked at Ben. 'Um—I take it it is OK for us to stay? I mean, just for a while? A few days or so? You will say if it isn't, or whatever—'

'Liv, it's fine; don't stress. I'll come up and give you a hand. What shall I bring?'

She looked at the things, then at Kit finally asleep wedged in cushions on one of the big chairs by the window, and shrugged. 'Nappies—both sorts. Nothing else. They'll sleep once they're in bed—please God.'

'I've got a cot—in case friends stay. It's not made up but it soon can be. Which one do you want to put in it?'

'Missy,' she said definitely, her mind at rest about the stairs now she knew her little daughter wouldn't be able to fall down them. 'Kit can sleep in a drawer or something.'

'So you can shut it if he screams?' Ben asked

mildly, leading her into a bedroom, the baby in his arms.

Liv laughed, the tension easing a fraction. 'Don't tempt me,' she said.

They went straight to sleep, Missy in the cot and Kit beside her in his makeshift little bed in the huge bottom drawer of a mahogany wardrobe, and Ben led Liv back downstairs, put a mug of tea in her hand and sat down, legs sprawled out under the kitchen table.

'Drink your tea,' he ordered, and she sat and picked up the mug, playing with it while she ran through the night again in her mind.

He said nothing, just watched her, and after a moment Liv stood up, mug in hand, and walked over to the window. It faced the road, beyond the curving drive and the neatly trimmed shrubs and the manicured lawn.

Liv didn't see them. What she saw was Oscar, arrogant, cocky, bored, telling her where he'd been, and who with, in graphic and embarrassing detail.

'Aren't you going to ask?' she said to Ben, an edge in her voice.

'You'll tell me when you're ready,' he said gently.

She put the mug down, hugging her elbows and pacing round the kitchen. 'He's a—a—' she began.

'Bastard?'

'No, thanks to him and his liberated attitude—but yes, he's a bastard in the sense you mean. Oh, yes.'

Ben shrugged. 'He always has been. It's taken you four years to realise it. I don't know why you didn't cotton on sooner.'

'Nobody told me.'

'People tend to be circumspect,' he said, chasing a bubble in the top of his tea. 'Anyway, it was so obvious I couldn't believe you didn't notice.'

'Well, I didn't,' she sighed. 'Besides, he was wonderful to me at first—when I had a figure.'

Ben's mouth tightened and his blue eyes seemed to shoot sparks. She thought inconsequentially that it was just as well Oscar wasn't in the room, because Ben would kill him. It was a tempting thought.

'So what happened tonight?'

She picked her tea up and went over to the table, sitting down again restlessly. There was a bowl of sugar on the table, and she played with it, dribbling the grains off the spoon, watching it intently without seeing it. 'He was late. He came home after midnight—he hadn't said he was going to be late, so I'd waited with supper for him. It was ruined, of course, but he didn't want it. He'd eaten.'

'Alone?'

She snorted and rammed the spoon back in the sugar. 'Yeah, right. Oscar doesn't eat alone. Oscar doesn't do anything alone. No, he was with his mistress. The one he's been keeping for the past six months or so.' She felt bile rise in her throat, and grabbed another toffee, ripping the wrapper off and shoving it in her mouth angrily.

'Six months!' she muttered round the sweet. 'Damn him, he's had her there for six months, cosily installed in the block next to his office so he didn't even have to make the effort of commuting for his sex!'

She bit down on the toffee and growled furiously. 'Do you know what he said to me?' she raged, standing up again and waving her arms wildly. 'He said he wanted a real woman—one who knew how to

please a man. He said he was sick of my baggy stomach and my sagging—'

She broke off and took a deep breath. 'He said I
stank of baby sick and he was fed up with falling
over toys and nearly breaking his ankles and coming
home to screaming kids and a woman who was con-
stantly out of commission—as if I was a dishwasher
that was on the blink, for goodness' sake! I'm his
wife! Well, no, I'm not, because the toad wouldn't
marry me, but you know what I mean.'

'So what happened then?' Ben asked, prompting
her gently.

She caught her breath and sighed. 'I said if that
was the way he felt, there was no point in putting up
with him and his vile temper any longer, and I'd leave
in the morning. He said why wait, so I didn't. I got
the children out of bed and walked out.'

'Without your credit cards.'

'Without my credit cards,' she said wryly. 'That
was a tactical error. Apart from that, it was the best
thing I've done in years.'

She looked up at Ben and found him smiling.
'What? What now?' she demanded, sparks flying
again.

His smile widened. 'Good girl,' he said warmly.
'Well done. It's been a long time coming, Liv, but
well done.'

The tension drained out of her, and she picked up
her cup and emptied it. She was starving, she realised.
Starving, exhausted and safe. 'I don't suppose you've
got such a thing as toast, have you?' she asked, and
he chuckled.

'Why not?' he said mildly. 'It's almost breakfast
time. We might as well have breakfast.'

*   *   *

She slept like a log. It was after eleven before she woke to the sound of the baby screaming and Ben's soothing voice just outside her door.

'Liv? Are you decent?'

She slid up the bed and tugged the soft, thick quilt up under her arms. 'Yes—come in.'

The door swung open and Ben entered, dressed in the snug and well-loved jeans and comfy sweater he'd worn the night before—or that morning, if she was being realistic. She'd only been in bed three hours. He looked fresh as a daisy, recently showered if the short, damp hair was anything to go by, and she could see a few of the fair, springy strands dripping slightly. She smiled a greeting, and he walked towards her, Kit flailing in his arms. 'Hi. One baby, rather loudly demanding Mum.'

He propped him up against his shoulder and jostled him soothingly, and the contrast between the big man and the tiny child brought a lump to Liv's throat. His large hand cupped the back of the baby's head tenderly, cradling it next to his newly shaven cheek, and he crooned softly.

'Hush, my precious,' he murmured, and Liv wondered sadly why Ben was so good with him and Kit's own father had been so bitter and indifferent.

Certainly he'd never called him precious.

'Is he OK?' she asked guiltily. 'I didn't even hear him cry—I'm sorry.'

'That's all right, I was up anyway. He's fine. Just hungry, I think, and a bit uncertain about my nappy-changing skills. Missy's still sleeping.'

She reached out and took the baby from him, and without thinking pulled up the T-shirt he'd lent her and settled Kit's mouth over her nipple.

There was instant, blissful silence, and she looked up with a smile on her face to see Ben staring down at her breast, an unreadable expression in his sapphire eyes. After a stunned second he cleared his throat and turned away, and she closed her eyes and sighed. Damn. She hadn't meant to offend him. She just hadn't thought.

'Sorry—' she began, but he cut her off.

'Don't apologise, you haven't done anything,' he said abruptly. 'I'll leave you in peace. Do you want a drink? My sisters always demand tea when they're breastfeeding—they say they get thirsty.'

'Please—if it's not a nuisance.'

He hovered in the doorway, his eyes fixed firmly on her face. 'What about a bottle? Want me to make one up, or do you want to give it a chance?'

She looked down at her breasts, soft and pale, not blue-veined and taut as they had been when they were full of milk, and sighed. 'I don't know. I want to feed him if I can, but I don't want him hungry.'

'Why don't I make up a small bottle just in case, and I'll ring the doctor and ask if the midwife can come and talk to you?'

'It's the health visitor,' she corrected. 'The midwife only looks after you for the first ten days—and anyway, we'll be all right.'

'Nevertheless, perhaps she can give you some advice. I'll ring.'

And he left her alone with the baby. He suckled well, but he wasn't satisfied, she could tell. He fussed and whinged, and she had to use the bottle Ben had made up to settle him in the end.

And then the health visitor came, as if by magic, and was wonderful, giving her all sorts of sane advice which she desperately needed, because she'd bottle-fed Missy at Oscar's insistence and wasn't really confident in her ability to feed Kit.

'You'll be fine,' the woman assured her cheerfully. 'Drink lots, plug him in whenever he seems hungry, top him up with the bottle only if it's absolutely necessary so you can get some sleep, and you'll soon find you've got more milk than you know what to do with. And now I need a quick cuddle with him before I have to go.'

She took Kit from Liv, and made all sorts of admiring noises that Kit found fascinating while Liv sat there and wondered how long they could go on imposing on Ben and relying on his good nature. Missy was curled up next to her on the big wide chair, watching the health visitor and sucking her thumb, and every now and then her eyelids drooped.

Good. If she needed a nap, and the baby would go down for a while, she could have a serious talk with Ben about this housekeeping job. Not that she knew the first thing about housekeeping! She'd left home at nineteen, lived in a dreadful shared house on yoghurt and tomatoes until she'd met Oscar, and then moved in with him into a serviced flat where the most she'd had to do was rustle up the odd meal at the weekend, if they weren't out and felt too pinched to order in.

Apart from that all she could manage were salads—models didn't tend to concentrate very much on food. It was a bit like a eunuch planning a seductive evening with a beautiful woman, she supposed—too frustrating to consider.

So, not the best training ground, but she'd manage. She'd learn.

She'd have to.

Ben leant back in the chair in his study and listened to Liv singing softly to the children overhead. It was a curiously comforting sound, something sweet and gentle that touched some fundamental part of him and made him feel the world was a better place.

Then the singing stopped, drifting away, and was replaced by soft footfalls coming down the stairs. They hesitated outside his study, and he stood up and went to the door, pulling it open.

Liv was standing there, hand raised to knock, and he smiled at her, still warmed by her lullaby.

'Hi. Fancy a cup of tea?' he asked.

'I wanted to talk to you.'

He nodded. 'Can we do it over tea? I was just going to make a cup.'

'I'll make it.'

She turned on her heel and strode briskly down to the kitchen, filled the kettle and put it on, her actions busy and purposeful. Ben waited, settling himself in the comfy chair by the French window, looking out over the back garden. She'd get round to it when she was ready. You couldn't hurry Liv. She did things her way, he'd learned that over the years.

While he waited he looked at the garden, tidied up for the winter, a few odd leaves blowing defiantly across the lawn. He loved the kitchen, facing both ways as it did and spanning the house. It was the only room apart from his bedroom that did that, and it was his favourite room in the house. In the summer he could sit here with the doors open, or take his coffee outside to enjoy the sound of birds and the distant bustle of traffic. In the winter, it was warm and snug and cosy.

In truth he hardly used the other rooms unless he was entertaining, and recently he'd done less and less of that. He was sick of the soulless merry-go-round of social chit-chat and gossip-mongering, and now he entertained for business reasons alone, and then usually in a hotel or restaurant, in the absence of a decent cook.

Anything rather than have his private space invaded by strangers.

'About the job.'

He looked up with a start, and frowned at Liv. 'Job?'

'The housekeeper's job—you rang me a couple of weeks ago to congratulate me on having Kit, and mentioned that you were looking for someone.'

He thought of Mrs Greer who had been with him for years. For all her sterling qualities she couldn't cook, and he'd wanted to find someone to fill that slot without losing her as his cleaning lady. Still, with Liv and the babies there, she'd be much more stretched on the cleaning front, and if Liv needed the 'job' as a sop to her pride, so be it.

She'd have to cook for herself and the children, anyway, so cooking for him as well wouldn't add a great deal to the burden and would make her feel useful. Besides, it would make sure she stayed for a while, so he could keep an eye on her and look after her and the children so they didn't all end up in a worse mess.

And he'd have company.

He settled back against the chair and steepled his fingers. 'Tell me about your qualifications,' he said deadpan, and to his amazement she took him seriously. She coloured and straightened up, her mouth a determined line, and her eyes locked with his, the resolve in them terrifying.

'I don't have any,' she told him bluntly. 'But I'll learn. I'll read books and practise and try new things, and I won't kill you with salmonella or anything like that. I won't let you down, Ben.'

He sat up and leant towards her, a smile teasing at his lips. 'I'm convinced. You can start now. Where's that tea?'

She looked down into the pot that she'd been mashing vigorously for the past few minutes, and coloured again. 'Um—I'll make fresh. I seem to have mangled the tea bags.'

Ben stifled the laugh, closed his eyes and prayed that it wasn't an omen for his gastronomic future.

CHAPTER TWO

'WHAT about your things?' Ben asked, sipping his tea warily.

'Things?'

'You know—all the stuff you left at the flat. Your clothes, the children's clothes and equipment, your personal bits and pieces. When do you want to go and pick them up?'

'I can't,' she told him flatly. 'Oscar won't let me have them; he said so.'

Ben's mouth tightened and he dragged an impatient hand through his close-cropped hair, ruffling it yet again. 'You need your nursery equipment. The children need continuity—not Kit, particularly, but Missy. She needs her familiar toys and clothes around her. You need your clothes—you can't wear that pair of trousers for ever. And what about all the personal stuff? You must want that.'

Liv shrugged and buttered another piece of toast. Want them or not, it was beyond her to go back to the flat and demand that Oscar give her the things. 'Could you give me an advance on my salary? I can go and buy something second hand—'

'While Oscar sits on all your things? What's the point? What does he need them for?'

'Spite? A weapon? A lever, in case he decides he wants me back?' She bit into the toast, a late lunch because she hadn't got round to dealing with it after her rather strange morning, and glanced up at Ben.

23

He was looking thoughtful and rather serious. 'Would you go?' he asked. 'Back to Oscar—would you go? Do you want to?'

'No way,' she said firmly. 'Absolutely not. There is nothing Oscar can do that would entice me back, and anyway, he doesn't want us. He only wanted me while everyone could remember my name and I was a cover girl on the glossies. He doesn't give a damn now. I told you that.'

'Yes, you did,' he said softly, and drained his tea.

'I have to go out,' he went on. 'Will you be OK? I can let you have a car—I've got a little runabout I use if I have to park at an airport or the station—less nickable than the Mercedes. You're welcome to use it, and there's a remote control unit in it for the garage door and the gate. The keys are hanging up there on the board.'

She followed his finger and nodded. 'Thank you. I could go to the shops and buy food for supper—oh. I haven't got the baby seats.'

'We'll sort that out soon. If you need to go out ring my cleaning lady. She's very obliging and she babysits for my sisters. I'm sure she wouldn't mind. Mrs Greer—her number's on the board. Now, money,' he went on. 'I'd better give you a cashpoint card for my account—are you sure I can trust you with it?' he teased, but it hurt. Oscar vetted her credit card bills, queried her bank account and dished out housekeeping as if he were pulling his own teeth. He was only ever extravagant if it was her money, but that was long gone.

'Liv, I was joking,' he said softly, and his large, firm hand came out and enveloped hers, giving her a comforting squeeze. 'Buy whatever you need—if there's something you have to have today, get it. We can shop for all the stuff the children need tomorrow, so long as you've got enough to get by till then.'

'Don't you have to be at work?' she asked worriedly. 'I've messed up your night, now I'm messing up your day.'

'I work from home a lot—I've got computer links to the office via the fax and email, and anyway, I employ good staff. If I want to take a day off, I can.' He stood up. 'Take care. I'll be in touch. I'll have my mobile with me—ring if you need me.'

'Where are you going?' she asked before she could stop herself, and then hated herself for sounding so clingy and wet.

'London—last-minute business meeting. I won't be late. Don't worry about cooking; we'll pick something up when I get back. Just feed Missy. If you raid the kitchen, I'm sure you'll find something for her.'

He bent over and dropped a kiss on her cheek, just as she turned her head, and his lips brushed hers.

It was the lightest touch, the merest whisper of a kiss, but something happened inside her that had her staring at the door long after he'd gone through it to the garage and disappeared through the gates and up the quiet, tree-lined road.

She lifted her hand and laid her fingers flat against her lips, feeling them thoughtfully. She could still feel the imprint—could feel the warmth, the texture of his lips, firm yet soft, supple, tantalising. How strange, that a kiss from Ben could make her feel so—

What? Alive? Aware?

Cherished...?

*　　*　　*

Ben pulled into the underground car park, spoke to the security guard, slipped him a couple of notes and glided into the visitor's spot the man pointed to.

The lift was waiting, and he went up the three floors and emerged into a carpeted foyer. A leggy blonde beamed at him and unravelled her limbs, tugging her skirt seductively. 'Can I help you?' she purred.

'I'd like to see Oscar Harding, please.'

'Do you have an appointment?'

Ben dug out his most manipulative smile and shared it with the ditzy woman. 'I'm sure he'll be willing to see me—could you be a darling and tell him I'm here? It's Ben Warriner.'

She picked up the phone, and Ben scanned the doors around the foyer. None of them had Oscar's name on, but he would stake his life that the right door would have a plate on it announcing his importance. Oscar would never let it go unremarked, so it must be further away, along the corridor perhaps.

He turned his attention back to the one-sided conversation. 'A Mr Warriner's here to see you, Mr Harding—Ben Warriner? He said you'd want to see him—oh. Right. I'll tell him that.'

She cradled the phone and looked up with an awkward smile. He would hazard a guess Oscar had said something unprintable, and she was obviously unskilled in this form of diplomatic brush-off. 'I'm afraid he's tied up for the rest of the day,' she lied, her eyes not quite meeting his. 'He said to make an appointment, if you don't mind.'

'Unfortunately I do,' Ben said smoothly. 'I've come a long way, I'll see him now. Which room is he in?'

Her eyes flicked involuntarily towards the corridor,

and she looked even more uncomfortable. 'Oh—no, you can't. I'm sorry, he won't see you, Mr Warriner, not without an appointment. He doesn't see anyone—'

'I think you'll find he will.' He strode down the corridor, leaving the girl calling after him and frantically reaching for the phone. A pair of double doors blocked the corridor, and he palmed them out of the way and scanned the doors.

Bingo. Bold as brass and writ large, as he'd expected— 'OSCAR HARDING, MANAGING DIRECTOR'.

He turned the handle and thrust the door open, just as Oscar rose from behind his desk.

'Throwing your weight around, Warriner, and upsetting my staff?'

Ben smiled grimly, scanning the desk and noting the photographs of Liv and the children strategically placed to reflect well on him. 'My apologies. I wanted a word,' he told him. 'You've been refusing my calls, Oscar, making things difficult. I've been trying to get you all day.'

'I've been busy.'

'Aren't we all? I've had a few distractions in the last twenty-four hours, though—three, to be exact. It's made it a little difficult to concentrate.'

'I had a feeling she'd come to you,' Oscar said lazily. 'She always did run to Uncle Ben when things got hot.'

'Hot? I would say things got stone-cold, Oscar— not hot. So, are you going to have me thrown out?'

Oscar laughed and sat down again, waving at the chair opposite. 'Good heavens, no. We're both civilised men. Have a seat, Ben. What can I do for you?

Has she sent you to negotiate her grovelling return, like the prodigal wife?'

Ben stifled the retort, thrust his hands in his pockets and crossed to the window. He preferred to stand—it gave him more authority over this snake in the grass. Anyway, it wouldn't take long...

She was asleep when he got back, curled up in his favourite chair at the end of the kitchen, her lashes like black crescents against her pale cheeks. She looked as young as Missy, and his heart went out to her.

He crouched down and laid a gentle hand on her knee.

'Liv?'

Her lashes fluttered and lifted, and he reached out and brushed a lock of hair away from her eyes. 'Hi.'

She struggled upright. 'Hi. You're later than I thought you were going to be.'

'I got held up. I've been to see Oscar. We're going to collect your things in the morning.'

Her jaw dropped, and she collected herself and shook her head. 'Wha—how?'

He smiled slightly. 'Let's just say there are one or two things I know about that he'd like kept secret.'

Her jaw snapped shut, and she stood up, hugging her arms around her waist. 'So—what are we going to take? Doesn't he mind?'

'I didn't ask. As for what we're taking, everything that's yours or the children's that you want. I've ordered a van and two packers, and it'll be there at eleven tomorrow so you can go through the flat yourself and pick up anything you want to bring. You can decide what to do with everything once it's here—throw it out, if you like.'

'Or sell it. Loads of my clothes don't fit any more. I could sell them in a second-hand shop. The money might come in handy.'

'What about all the money you earned modelling?' Ben asked, puzzled. 'There must have been—well, I hate to think how much.'

She gave a bitter little laugh. 'Didn't you notice the flash cars and the furniture in the flat?'

'I haven't seen the flat. I went to the office.'

'That's even worse. He spent a fortune there "creating the right image". Don't worry, Ben, there's nothing left of my modelling money. Oscar's seen to that over the last four years.'

'You gave it to him?'

She snorted wryly. 'Not exactly gave. What do you think we lived on until it ran out? His business? I don't think so. It's been screeching and bumping along on the bottom for more years than I care to think about, but God forbid anyone should guess. I only found out by accident. We still had to project the right image, though. Some of my clothes were hideously expensive, but he thought it was justified—he saw me as the ultimate fashion accessory. I should be able to get quite a good price for them.'

But not enough to live on, Ben thought. Not by a country mile. Not ever. He found himself hating Oscar even more, and that galled him because it was such a waste of energy. He made himself concentrate on what mattered.

'How about supper? Are you hungry?' he asked.

She nodded. 'Starving—I had more toast when I

fed Missy, but I think it's all I've had in the last twenty four hours.'

'I'll order something—Chinese? Indian?'

'Can we have fish and chips?' she asked wistfully. 'I haven't had fish and chips out of the wrapper for years.'

'We'll have to do something about that, then,' he said with a smile. 'We'll get them locally tonight, and one day I'll take you up the coast to Aldeburgh and we'll get the best fish and chips you've ever tasted and eat them sitting on the sea wall.'

He went back out, drove to the nearest decent chippy and went home to enjoy the satisfying sight of Liv, cross-legged in one of the chairs, tucking into the impromptu meal with great concentration. Ben was fascinated. He'd never seen anyone before eat with such dedicated single-mindedness. She didn't even pause for breath.

Then she screwed up the paper, licked her fingers one by one and grinned. 'Wow. That was the best.'

He chuckled and relieved her of the wrapper, putting it with his into the bin. 'I thought you models only ate raw tomatoes and lettuce leaves.'

She wrinkled her nose. 'I know. Millions of calories, but I don't care. I was so hungry. I can diet tomorrow.'

'You don't need to diet.'

'Oh, I do,' she corrected. 'I'm much fatter than I used to be.'

She was. Personally, Ben thought it was a huge improvement. He didn't like skinny, anorexic-looking women. He liked smooth curves and soft hollows and firm, substantial limbs. He liked a woman that didn't feel as if she would break if he touched her.

He looked at Liv, pottering at the sink now, washing her hands and filling the kettle, and frowned thoughtfully. Had Oscar made her feel unhappy about her body? He thought it quite likely, from the odd remarks she'd made about breastfeeding.

He shook his head slowly. He'd had to restrain himself hard today to keep from punching the guy's lights out. The last thing he needed was any more reasons to go back to London and satisfy that urge. Thankfully Oscar was going to be out of the way tomorrow—that was one of the conditions.

Ben thought he'd put the frighteners on him sufficiently that he wouldn't be a problem. If not, he had a few other tricks up his sleeve. He'd been watching the sleaze ball for the last four years, ever since he'd latched on to Liv, and he'd acquired quite a body of information. The man had a respectable veneer about a millimetre thick, and under that he was all slime. Ben just hoped Liv never had to find out quite how bad he really was.

It was odd going back. They'd left the children in the care of Ben's cleaning lady, a sweet and motherly sort whom Liv had trusted instantly. The journey to London had been uneventful in Ben's Mercedes, and she'd had nothing to take her mind off Oscar and what he would say.

'Are you sure he's not going to be there?' she asked for the hundredth time as they turned into the underground car park, and Ben shot her a patient and understanding smile.

'Quite sure. Stop worrying, Liv, it'll be all right.'

It was. There was no sign of Oscar, just an empty flat that echoed with memories, most of them unpleasant. The packers were quick and efficient, and within half an hour all trace of her life there had been removed. She had the baby photos, all her modelling memorabilia and the childhood bits and pieces that she'd brought from her parents' house, and all the children's things.

And her clothes, wonderful clothes that would never fit her again, extravagant designer originals and exquisitely tailored suits and dresses. She looked down at her jeans and jumper that she'd changed into, and sighed.

Her life was going to be very different from now on, but she had no regrets. Leaving Oscar was the best and most sensible thing she'd done in the last four years.

'Right, I'm done,' she said to Ben, and he nodded. 'Right, that's it, lads, thank you. See you in Suffolk.'

They went out, and she took one last look round.

'Sad?' Ben asked her, and she shook her head.

'Absolutely not. I feel nothing. It's actually quite scary.'

He put his arm round her and hugged her up against his solid, dependable warmth. 'Come on, let's go home,' he said, and she really felt as if that was what she was doing.

Going home.

Missy was thrilled to see her toys again. Her little face lit up, and Liv was glad she'd gone back with Ben and collected everything. There were so many treasures, as well—things like Missy's first haircut, and the baby photos. She wouldn't have been able to bear losing the baby photos, and she didn't imagine

Oscar would miss them. She'd send him copies, but it was probably pointless.

He'd got photos of them on his desk, in silver frames—if they were still there. It was all for show, of course—all part of his 'trust me' image. The perfect father of the perfect children.

They were being less than perfect at that moment, Missy crying because she couldn't make a piece of her jigsaw fit the wrong way round, and Kit because he'd woken up and was suddenly, furiously hungry.

She helped Missy with the errant bit of jigsaw, picked the baby up out of his crib and settled down into the chair to feed him. He was impatient and screamed again, but as soon as she pulled her jumper out of the way, unclipped her bra and settled him at her breast, there was a blissful silence broken only by the occasional slurp as he suckled.

She closed her eyes, settled back against the comforting embrace of the big chair and felt her shoulders drop with the release of tension. She ought to be thinking about the evening meal—taking her housekeeping duties seriously—but she had to feed the baby and for now, what she needed was peace. Peace and—

'Tea?'

She looked up to find Ben there, eyes carefully not on her breasts, not that there was a lot to see with her jumper drooping down and the baby's head in the way, but it did seem to make him strangely uncomfortable. Still, he was there, rendering first aid as if he'd read her mind, and she loved him for it. He was a wonderful friend.

'Please,' she said, smiling. 'He's starving. Mrs

Greer said he wouldn't take his bottle very well this morning. Perhaps he's getting used to me again.'

'Hope so. It's good for you both—just what you need. Oh, Missy, won't it fit?'

He crouched down beside her daughter, and gently and patiently helped her complete the jigsaw. When it was done she picked up the wooden puzzle and waved it triumphantly, and all the pieces fell out. She giggled and picked them up, and she and Ben put them back again while Liv watched, entranced.

The kettle boiled, and he made some tea and sat in the other chair, bending forwards sometimes to help Missy, and at other times focusing on his mug of tea with undue concentration.

Still avoiding looking at her, she realised, and chewed her lip. It obviously worried him.

'Would you be happier if I fed the baby upstairs, out of your way?' she asked quietly. 'I mean, I don't want to embarrass you.'

He turned his head, meeting her eyes, and then lowered them, looking at the baby, at her breast, at the rosebud mouth suckling vigorously at her nipple. Then he raised his head and met her eyes again, and there was something unreadable and curiously sad in them.

'You don't embarrass me, Liv,' he said, and his voice was gruff and tender. 'You go ahead and feed him wherever you like.'

He looked away, returning his attention to his tea, and she gave a tiny shrug and eased the baby off, burping him and swapping sides. It was getting easier, she realised—more natural. Practice was obviously making perfect, or something closer to it, at least. And now Ben had assured her he wasn't embarrassed, she relaxed again.

He must be right. If he was embarrassed, he'd take himself off to his study instead of actively seeking her out and having tea with her. Perhaps he'd just been avoiding looking at her because he didn't want to embarrass *her*, rather than the other way round.

She gave up worrying and concentrated on the tiny, downy head snuggled in the crook of her arm. So soft, so fragile and vulnerable, and yet so very good at getting his own way. Nature, she decided with satisfaction, was immensely clever.

'I've put the baby seats in the car for you,' he said out of the blue, 'so when you want to go out, they're all ready. Do you want a buggy in the car too?'

She was still dealing with nature being clever, and she looked at him blankly. 'Go out?' she said, like an idiot.

'Yes—out. You know—shopping and things?'

Buying food for his supper. Oh, Lord.

'Great. Thanks,' she said, and conjured up a smile. 'What do you fancy eating tonight?'

'What can you cook?' he asked, and her mind went totally blank.

Not hard. On the culinary front, her mind *was* totally blank. Well, not totally, but it certainly wasn't her strongest point.

'Um—chicken in sauce?'

'Sounds promising. What sort of sauce?'

Bottled, she nearly said, but one look at his hopeful face and she stifled the retort. 'I don't know. I haven't thought. Rice or potatoes?'

'Rice.'

'OK.' Blast. Rice was tricky. Even she could scrub

potatoes and put them in the oven, but rice was the one thing that had always defeated her. Why on earth had she suggested it? Idiot. Still, boil in the bag, that was the thing. Idiot-proof.

Kit had finished his feed, and she laid him on her lap, restored her modesty and stood up. 'I'll change him—Missy, do you want to come with me?'

She shook her head. 'Puzzle,' she said, and looked hopefully at Ben. 'Help,' she ordered, and to her astonishment he got down on his hands and knees on the rug and helped her.

'Like mother, like daughter,' he murmured. 'Twisting me round your little finger—I don't know. Talk about manipulated.'

Missy giggled, and he pressed her nose and made a noise. She giggled again, and Liv tore herself away and went upstairs to change the baby's nappy. With any luck he'd sleep through their shopping trip and not be too much of a nuisance...

He screamed. He screamed from the moment she walked through the door of the supermarket, with him in his nest in the newborn cradle on the trolley and Missy beside him in the toddler seat.

He screamed through the vegetables, past the dairy products, up and down the baby aisle and through the chiller section. He let up for a minute in the frozen food aisle, then started again in the biscuits.

Liv gave up. She'd bought a bottle of sauce to add to chicken for a casserole, she'd bought chicken breast fillets, boil-in-the-bag rice, frozen peas and sweetcorn. She'd found food for Missy, something instant and delicious-looking for dessert and that would have to do.

She headed home, getting lost once on the way because she wasn't very good at doing directions backwards and Kit was making it hard to concentrate, and when she arrived back at the house it was deserted.

She felt a curious pang of disappointment. She'd expected Ben to be here, and she'd grown rather used to his company in the past two days. Silly, really, because he had work to do and between them they must be playing havoc with his schedule, but the house seemed horribly empty without him.

She brought the children in, settled Kit in the crib in the kitchen and left him to scream for a moment while she brought the rest of the things in from the car. Fortunately the garage was large and attached to the house, so it was easy to carry things through with Missy milling around under her feet in perfect safety.

Well, almost perfect. She stumbled down the step and grazed her hands, and screamed even louder than Kit, and Liv cuddled her and washed her hands and wondered how on earth she was going to get a chance to cook.

She cuddled the baby again, settled him at last and turned her attention to supper. She studied the instructions on the side of the jar, decided they looked foolproof and stopped worrying. What could go wrong?

'Right, little Miss, are you going to help me?' she asked. Missy nodded, and Liv lifted her up and sat her on the edge of the worktop next to the sink, and washed and dried all four of their hands. Then she settled her in her high chair without the tray, fastened the lapstrap and pushed her up to the edge of the kitchen table so she could join in.

'Now, first things first; read the instructions again,' she said, and Missy reached for the jar.

'No, I'll have it, darling, please. I don't want it to break; it's my only chance of impressing him. Now. Cut the chicken up, put it in a casserole dish, pour sauce over. Bake. Easy-peasy,' she said with a grin, and Missy giggled.

'Shall I cut up the chicken?' Missy nodded, then watched intently as she cubed it neatly and spread it in the bottom of the dish. 'Now, the sauce,' she said, and picked up the jar.

The lid wouldn't shift. She ran it under hot water, gripped it with a tea towel and finally it came away with a pop.

She turned back to Missy, and saw to her horror that she had escaped from her high chair and was sitting on the table, playing with the sugar bowl. 'How did you get out?' she asked in amazement, and Missy gave her a megawatt smile.

'Missy undo it,' she piped proudly. 'Missy clever.'

One more thing to worry about! Liv thought with a slightly desperate laugh, and scooped her errant daughter off the table, removing the sugar bowl from her grasp. At least there wasn't too much in there! It could have gone everywhere, and instead there was just a little sprinkle here and there. 'As if I didn't have enough to worry about—stay there, please!' she instructed, strapping her firmly back into the chair.

She stayed, while Liv poured the sauce quickly over the chicken, spread it evenly and stuck it in the oven.

While it cooked she made Missy scrambled eggs and chopped up bacon, with toast fingers and a glass of fruit juice, and fed Kit again before bathing them both and popping them into bed. Then she cooked the rice, fluffed it up, left it to keep warm in the other oven and boiled the veg while she laid the table.

The gateau was thawing, the children were in bed asleep, the table was laid—success.

Feeling thoroughly pleased with herself, she settled back to wait for Ben.

It was revolting. She hadn't expected it to be nice, but it was bizarre. Sickly.

Liv pushed her plate away and looked up at Ben in disgust. 'I'm sorry. I thought it would be OK—it sounded nice. I can't believe the sauce is so awful.'

She prodded the rice disparagingly. It was lovely, but it had been soaked with the sauce, and—well, frankly it was horrible.

The chicken underneath had been all right, but the jar of sauce had been more than generous, and it was hard to find any chicken without it.

Ben was shuffling it round his plate, tasting it cautiously, his brow furrowed. 'Um—is it by any chance supposed to be sweet and sour?' he ventured. 'Perhaps—without the sour?'

Sweet and—?

'Oh, no!' She clapped her hand over her mouth and stared at Ben in horror.

He froze, his fork halfway to his mouth, his expression comical. 'What?' he asked warily.

'Missy,' she said, remembering. 'I couldn't get the lid off, and when I did, she'd escaped from her high chair and she was paddling in the sugar bowl on the table.'

'Anywhere near the chicken?'

She nodded miserably. 'It was just there, beside

her. She was helping me. She must have tipped it on to the chicken—oh, Ben, I'm sorry!'

'Or were you trying to sweeten me up?' he said mildly, pushing his plate away.

'Wretched child,' she said crossly, throwing the ruined meal into the bin. 'I'll kill her.'

'No, you won't,' he said. 'You'll keep it out of her way in future—if there's going to be a future. I thought you said you could cook?' he added teasingly.

'I said I could learn—and I only promised you wouldn't get salmonella,' she reminded him. 'I never said you'd like it.'

His mouth twitched, and she cleared the plates away and sighed. 'Dare I ask about a dessert?' he said from behind her. She had the feeling he was getting ready to duck, in case she threw something at him. She stifled a smile.

'Not had enough sugar yet?' she teased, and he growled softly. She laughed and patted his cheek consolingly. 'You're all right. I bought a chocolate gateau. I didn't think even I could ruin it, unwrapping it, and I promise you Missy hasn't been near it!'

He chuckled, and she put the gateau and their plates down on the table with a pot of cream, a knife and two spoons, and between them they ate it all. At least he didn't seem angry, Liv thought, and wondered yet again why a man as genuinely nice as Ben still wasn't married. The girls in Suffolk must all need their heads checked, she decided.

'Do you think a cup of normal coffee to finish is expecting too much, or should I resign myself to Turkish?' Ben asked wryly, and she chuckled and flapped him with a teatowel.

'Don't push your luck. Where do you want it?'

'In the drawing room? I hardly ever use it, but it's a nice room. Or my study. That's cosier, but it'll remind me of all the work I should be doing.'

'Or we could stay here. I love those chairs.'

His eyes crinkled. 'Me, too. Let's do that.'

He helped her clear up, and when the coffee was done they settled down in the chairs with a sigh and talked about nothing in particular for hours.

They'd always been able to talk, she mused as she fed Kit in her room just before she went to bed. In all the years she'd known him, they'd never been lost for words, or awkward, or distant.

Well, only once.

When she'd told him she was moving in with Oscar. Then he'd been distant, and she had the strangest feeling he'd been hurt, but she couldn't imagine why. He had no interest in her—if he had had, he would have said so, and he always seemed to have a bevy of girlfriends hanging round him like bees round a honeypot.

It was the only time in ten years that she'd felt that he disapproved of her, and it had hurt her terribly. She'd treasured his friendship ever since she and her parents had moved in next to his family when she was fifteen and he was twenty-two. He'd been away at university and had come back, and was working in his father's firm.

They'd moved in the same circles, mixed with the same people, and she'd always known she was too young to interest him, but he'd been endlessly kind to her and patiently escorted her to a host of parties. Then, when she'd grown older, he'd been just the same, good old Ben, her best friend and confidant.

He'd taught her to drive, taken her out to celebrate when she'd passed her test, and again when she got her first major modelling job.

She'd dropped out of university to pursue her career, and he'd turned up one day on the set of a shoot and taken her out to lunch. He was there for her when she'd had her first disastrous affair, and he'd never criticised or interfered.

Till Oscar. Then, he'd just taken himself away for a while, and she'd missed him horribly.

She wondered if he even realised she was a woman and not just a person, and then she laughed at herself. How many of her friends had wailed that their partners didn't realise they were people and not just women? And she was complaining that Ben was the other way round.

Well, not complaining. Of course not. She and Ben were very dear and close friends, nothing more, nothing less, and she knew that he would never see her as anything else. Not after all this time.

It was a curiously saddening thought.

CHAPTER THREE

THE following day she put the children in the double buggy, warmly wrapped up and covered with the hood, just in case it rained, and headed off to the centre of Woodbridge.

There was an up-market second-hand shop there that dealt in nearly-new designer clothes, and when she told them what she had to sell, the owner was ecstatic. 'May I come round, to save you dragging everything down here? I can go through them with you and tell you what will sell.'

'OK,' she agreed, hugely relieved that she wasn't going to have to struggle with the clothes and the children.

'It's coming up to the ball season, as well—have you got any evening wear?'

'Masses,' Liv assured her drily. 'Are there any skinny women in Woodbridge?'

'Lots,' she said with a laugh. 'I hate them all. When would you like me to come? Day or evening?'

'Day's better,' Liv said, thinking of Ben coming home from work and the chaos of supper and bath-time, and they arranged a time the following day. Then Liv strolled up the main street, window shopping, and thinking what a pleasant, pretty town it was. She went into the chemist and bought vitamins for the children, and then couldn't resist the bread shop.

They had big hedgehog loaves in the window, and

43

Missy screamed because they weren't for sale and she couldn't get one.

'Never mind. We can make one,' she promised rashly, and was wondering how on earth she could achieve it when she clashed wheels with another buggy.

'Sorry,' she said, smiling, and looked up to see the familiar face of Kate, an old college friend, staring at her in amazement.

'Liv? Liv Kensington? What are you doing here?'

'Shh,' she said with a smile, conscious that her name, if not her face, would attract attention. Nobody would notice a woman with two children, but her name had once been as well known as Liz Hurley's, and she didn't want to be reminded—not when she was two stone overweight and her hair was on end! 'I'm staying here for a while with a friend. What about you, Kate? You look wonderful! Tell me all about yourself.'

Kate laughed. 'Nothing to tell. I'm married to Andy—you remember Andy, he was around at college—and I've got three children—these are the youngest—and I live in Woodbridge. Where are you staying?'

She told Kate the address, and her jaw dropped. 'But that's next door but one! We're neighbours! How amazing. You must come round—what are you doing now?'

Liv shrugged. 'Nothing. I have to get back because Kit's going to wake up soon, and he'll scream all the way home.'

'Why don't you come round?' Kate offered. 'Have coffee with me—or lunch. Both. We can catch up. That would be so good.'

So they pushed their buggies back up the hill, and she went into Kate's chaotic but friendly kitchen, and while Kate made coffee she fed Kit and watched the children playing together. Missy was thrilled to have new toys to look at, and there was a smidgen of hope that she'd forget the hedgehog bread!

'So you're staying with Ben, are you?' Kate said, settling down at the table for a good gossip. 'Do tell all! How come your hubby's let you slip the leash and stay with a guy like that? He must need his head examined! Andy gets the hump if Ben so much as sets foot on the drive while he's out—he says all that testosterone is bound to go to my head!'

She laughed good-naturedly, and Liv gave a polite chuckle.

Testosterone? Ben?

Was she missing something—or had that shiver of awareness when his lips had accidentally clashed with hers been more than just a fluke?

'I don't have a husband,' she confessed, dragging her mind back to Kate's question. 'Oscar and I never got married.'

'Oh, Lord, Oscar Harding—I remember reading about you in one of the glossies. But that was years ago!'

'Four,' she confessed with a wry smile. 'I'm old news now.'

'Four years. Heavens. I suppose it would be; I was at home with Jake. That was how I had time to read a magazine, I guess! Wow. I never thought I'd see you again. So where's Oscar now?'

She shrugged. 'In London. I've left him.'

'With the babies and everything? Gosh, I expect he was gutted.'

Liv gave a hollow laugh. 'No. Not gutted. Not Oscar.'

'Oh, love, I'm sorry,' Kate said sincerely. 'So how will you cope?'

She laughed again, with more humour this time. 'I'm Ben's new housekeeper,' she admitted. 'He's being more than kind. I cannot cook to save my life, and it doesn't help when Missy puts sugar in the chicken casserole.'

Kate's jaw dropped, and then she laughed till the tears ran down her face. 'Oh, no. I'm sorry, I have this dreadful vision—'

'It's probably accurate,' Liv said with another wry smile. 'It was awful. It probably would have been pretty awful without Missy's help, though, to be fair.'

Kate sat back and tipped her head on one side. 'Want me to teach you? I mean, say no if you don't, but really there are some dead easy things that will impress the socks off him. I've got a long list of them—I use one of them on Andy if I want something.' She grinned mischievously. 'I do a great line in aphrodisiacs,' she stage-whispered, and Liv smiled ruefully.

'I don't need aphrodisiacs. He's just a friend.'

Kate's eyes widened. 'Really?' she said. 'What a wicked waste! Oh, well. You could try. While there's life, there's hope.'

Liv shook her head. 'No. Sorry to disappoint you—but yes, please, I'd love you to teach me how to cook. I need this job.'

Kate started there and then with her own supper menu for that night. 'I'll give it to you for lunch and I'll do something else for Andy—then you can go home and do it for Ben and he'll be dead impressed.

Now, the important thing to remember is, don't panic, and don't make the sauce too hot.'

She didn't get a chance to cook for him that night, because he came home and said he was having to go out again. He disappeared to his room, and emerged half an hour later showered and changed. She sniffed appreciatively.

'Nice aftershave.'

'Chanel. I like it—it's not sweet.'

She arched a brow and said nothing, and he grinned. 'Right. Time for dinner.'

'I don't believe this is business. You're just frightened of my cooking,' she said dolefully, and he laughed and hugged her to his side.

'Poor Liv,' he teased. 'Still, you can slob around in front of the television and relax without worrying about me. And don't wait up; I'll probably be late. It's a haulage company that want me to deal with them—they're trying to sweeten me up.'

'I'll lend them Missy, shall I?' she said wryly, and he chuckled.

'No—I want to enjoy my meal. Have an early night. You're looking tired. You've had a lot of stress in the last few days—chill out for a while. I'll see you tomorrow.'

And he went, brushing his lips over her brow and leaving her with the lingering, slightly lemony scent of his aftershave teasing her nostrils.

The house felt incredibly empty.

She tried Kate's dish the next night, Saturday, but she forgot Kate's instructions and must have overheated the sauce because it separated and went funny.

'It tastes lovely,' Ben said generously, ignoring the texture and appearance.

Liv was less forgiving. 'It feels gritty. It must be the yoghurt—I got it too hot.'

'It's better than the chicken was,' he assured her, and she smiled bravely and served him another dead cert pudding from the freezer cabinet of the supermarket as a reward for not being critical.

Actually, over the next couple of weeks her culinary skills continued to improve. Kate's recipes were easy, as she'd promised, but what Liv found impossible—what she'd always found impossible—was ignoring the children in order to prepare the meals and do the housework.

Not that she had a lot of housework to do, because Mrs Greer came in three times a week and did the majority, but Missy seemed to leave a trail of havoc behind her, and Liv was paranoid about the mess because of Oscar being so horrible about it. The last thing she wanted was to upset Ben, too, and so she tried desperately to keep the mess confined to the end of the kitchen, on and around the rug by the chairs.

It meant Missy could play under her supervision, so she managed to do some of the food preparation during the day, but she found she was resorting to frozen vegetables for speed and ease.

Ben, bless his heart, never complained, and he was always nice to Missy, but there were days when he came in and shut himself in his study, and they always seemed to be the days when things had gone wrong and the place was out of control.

Like Friday, a little over two weeks since she'd arrived. He came in, looked round, sighed and went into the study with hardly a word.

'Do you want a cup of tea?' she called after him.

'Please. Sorry, I've got work to do.'

She took him the tea and he grunted his thanks and carried on with his work, and she went back to the kitchen feeling like a whipped puppy and berating herself for being so stupid.

She was employed as his housekeeper, for goodness' sake! Just because they'd been friends for years that didn't mean he had to rush into the kitchen and spend the rest of the evening with her, or invite her to curl up in his study for a cosy chat!

Maybe he really did have work to do. Maybe it was nothing to do with the mess.

'And maybe pigs fly,' she muttered, just as he came into the room behind her.

'Not in this neck of the woods,' he told her. 'Why are they flying?'

She flapped a hand at him, waving him away. 'Nothing. What's the matter, is the tea too weak?'

'No, it's fine,' he said with a lazy grin, propping his hips against the worktop and getting in the way. 'I'm bored with work. I thought I'd let it wait and come and have a chat instead. How's your day been?'

So much for her paranoia!

'OK,' she lied. Actually Kit had been restless, Missy had been clingy and whining, probably because of Kit, and she'd managed to get nothing done at all. And the kitchen, his favourite room in the house, so he'd told her, looked as if a bomb had gone off in it.

Ben didn't look as if he cared. He looked his usual cheerful, easy-going self, and she wondered what on earth she'd done to deserve him.

Put up with Oscar for four years, probably. A girl had to have some breaks. 'I'm sorry about the mess,' she said, feeling guilty anyway. 'I was just going to clear up. The time ran away with me.'

'That's OK,' he said easily. 'Want a hand with the meal?'

There was a wail from upstairs, and she sighed and looked at him. 'It's all right. Let me sort Kit out, and I'll come down and do it. Are you in a hurry?'

He shook his head. 'No, no hurry. I just thought you might like some company—and it might justify me not being in my study working!'

'I'll bring Kit down if he's hungry—you can make me a cup of tea,' she said with an impish grin. 'That'll give you a valid excuse to avoid your study.'

She ran up and picked the baby out of his cot, cradling him against her shoulder. 'What's the matter, sweetheart?' she crooned softly. 'Are you hungry?'

His little mouth pecked at her neck, seeking for sustenance, and she carried him down to the kitchen, settled herself in a chair and started feeding him.

Ben brought her tea, looked down at her for a second and then cleared his throat. 'I've got to make a call. I'd forgotten. I'll be back in a minute.'

Liar, she thought, and was suddenly saddened. She thought they'd got past the stage of him avoiding her when she was feeding Kit, but apparently not. She sighed wearily and smoothed the baby's downy head. He was growing fast, gaining weight and getting much longer. He'd need to move up to the next size of sleepsuit soon.

He was six weeks old already. In a way it felt like five minutes, and in another way, because of all that had happened since his birth, it felt like years.

Oscar had been mercifully silent, and Liv didn't think she'd hear from him again. It was no great loss.

She didn't think he'd want to keep in touch with the children, and after what he'd said, she didn't feel he deserved them. Already, in two and a half weeks, Ben had been more of a father to the two of them than Oscar had ever been.

She realised that she ought to go to the doctor and have her post-natal check-up, to make sure everything was back to normal after the birth, but there didn't seem any urgency. She knew she was well, and Kit was thriving. Still, they probably should register with the doctor up here—

'Is he all right?'

She glanced up at Ben, standing in the doorway, his face shadowed. 'Yes, he's fine. Made your call?'

'He's out. I'll try later. More tea?'

She nodded, and he took the mug from her, carefully avoiding looking at Kit this time. She burped him and swapped sides while Ben poured her tea, and made sure her jumper was artfully arranged to give him nothing to get upset about.

A friend of hers had used a shawl draped over her shoulder and the baby's head, to give her privacy, and it was a good idea. Liv thought she might try it. She had a shawl somewhere in all her things.

'There's a party tomorrow night,' Ben said, easing himself down into the other chair and looking down into his tea. 'I have to go—it's a company do. I wondered if you'd like to come—you always used to like parties.'

In the days, Liv thought, when she could lie in till twelve! 'What about the baby?'

'We don't have to be long. It starts at eight and finishes at midnight—we could do nine to eleven, or

something like that. Fancy it? Mrs Greer could probably babysit.'

She chewed her lip thoughtfully. 'What about
clothes? How formal is it? I don't know what I've
got in the way of formal that would fit me since Kit.
I've got rather more bust than I used to have.'

He flicked an involuntary glance at her chest and
looked away again hastily. 'Um—yes, you probably
have. Not that formal, I don't think. It's probably
black tie, though. Do you have anything?'

'I might. It would be rather nice to go out—I
haven't been out for ages—probably nearly a year.
Oscar didn't like me being seen when I was pregnant.
He wasn't into fecundity—a bit too earthy and vulgar
for him.'

Ben gave a humourless snort of laughter. 'He really
was a toad to you, wasn't he?'

She shrugged. 'He didn't really want the children,
he was humouring me—or keeping me quiet so he
could indulge himself with his mistress and still get
access to my money, more likely. Only, of course, it
ran out.'

She sighed heavily. 'I could have done with it to
support the children, but I don't have any rights in
law. He'd just say I'd squandered it, and he'd be right.
I did—on him. Still, it's over now.'

'Do you want some money to buy a dress for tomorrow?' he asked her softly. 'I could babysit while
you go shopping.'

'You won't get anything done,' she warned him.
'Missy's a full-time job.'

He laughed wryly. 'I've noticed. My sisters have
toddlers, Liv. I know about them. Don't worry, they'll

be quite safe. Kit might get hungry, but they won't come to any harm.'

She looked down at the baby, sleeping now, his little mouth soft against her nipple. Every now and then he sucked reflexively, then relaxed again, his tiny jaw drooping. She smiled and smoothed his head, then lifted him away and pulled her jumper down.

'Fancy a cuddle?' she asked Ben, and he nodded and held out his arms.

'He might throw up on you,' she warned. 'I haven't burped him.'

'I can cope. The shirt needs washing anyway—on the subject of which, I don't suppose you're going to do a white wash, are you? My dress shirt's in the laundry basket and I'll need it for tomorrow. I've got another one but I don't like it as much.'

'I'll do it for you now,' she said, and went upstairs. His laundry basket was bulging, and she felt a pang of guilt. It was one of her jobs, and one she'd been neglecting. She sorted through it for white things, stuffed everything else back in with a promise to do it the next day, gathered up the armful of whites and went downstairs again.

Ben and Kit were nose to nose, the baby staring intently at him, Ben making silly faces.

'You'll scare him,' she said drily, and he chuckled.

'I don't think so. He's made of sterner stuff than that, aren't you, little mate?'

She went into the utility room, shoved the clothes into the washing machine and switched it on. By the time she went back into the kitchen, Kit was settled again in the crook of Ben's arm, sleeping peacefully, and Ben looked relaxed and very much the proud father.

Liv felt a sudden pang of regret that he wasn't, and then chided herself for being so silly. Theirs wasn't that sort of relationship. It was unthinkable.

It was a great shame, because if she could have designed herself a house and husband to fit her dreams, this house and this man would have come impossibly close to a perfect match.

She sighed, and Ben glanced up at her. 'Tired?' he asked gently.

She nodded. 'I am a bit. He was restless last night. I think I might have an early night after supper.'

'Why don't I order something in?' he suggested. 'It would save you having to cook.'

She shook her head. 'No. You're paying me to be your housekeeper, and I'm doing almost nothing. It's not fair.'

'Whoever said anything about fair?' he murmured. 'Why don't we have scrambled eggs on toast?' he went on. 'I can make it while you put the baby to bed.'

She gave him a grateful smile. 'That sounds wonderful, actually,' she confessed. 'I've just remembered I haven't taken anything out of the freezer. I meant to, earlier, but the day just...' She shrugged.

'Ran away with you? I know the feeling. Put Kit to bed and come down and let me spoil you a little. I think you've earned it.'

She wasn't going to argue any more. She was bushed, and if he wanted her to scintillate and look good tomorrow night, she was going to have to get some sleep.

She had nothing in her wardrobe that would fit. In desperation she collared Ben. 'I'd like to slip into town for a few minutes—you couldn't watch the children, could you?' she asked, and he nodded.

'Of course—I said I would.'

'I won't be long,' she promised, and went to the nearly-new shop to see if any of her clothes had been sold. The lady told her delightedly that almost everything had gone.

'Could I have a look through the evening wear? I've got to go out tonight and nothing fits me since I had the baby. Perhaps you could deduct it from what you owe me?'

'Certainly. Go and have a look. Actually some new things have just come in late yesterday, and I haven't had time to put them out. The lady lives in London and comes up at the weekend sometimes to visit her mother—she doesn't like to sell her things in her home patch, so you're unlikely to bump into her. She's about your size.'

She was, and she had brought in a lovely dress, with a high draped neck at the front, scooping down at the back in soft folds to just above her bra strap. It was black, very simple, and it was beautifully cut. It fitted Liv like a dream.

'I'll have it,' she said rashly, ignoring the hole it was making in her profit. She had other things to sell, and she wanted to look her best. Ben had been so kind to her she didn't want to let him down by looking like a frump.

'Are you all right for shoes?'

She nodded. 'I've got tons of shoes. It's only my bust really that's changed—and my waist, and my hips,' she added with a laugh. 'Perhaps it's only my feet that haven't.'

'Well, you look wonderful in the dress, anyway,'

the woman told her. 'I hope you have a lovely time tonight. By the way, I don't suppose you've got any other things you'd like to bring in, have you?'

'I'll look some out,' Liv promised.

The woman gave her a cheque for the clothes she'd sold, less the cost of the new dress, and Liv went home via the bank, paying the cheque into her account with a feeling of relief.

She could sell her jewellery, as well. Some of that was valuable, and she didn't need it. Security for her children seemed suddenly much more important, and she wasn't going to let vanity or sentiment get in her way.

Ben was in the kitchen when she got back, walking up and down with Kit cradled against his shoulder. The baby was crying intermittently, and as she went down the hall, the thick carpet muffling her footfalls, she could hear him talking to Kit, his voice low and soothing. She couldn't hear the words, but they were irrelevant. It was his tone that was calming the fractious baby—his tone and the gentle, steady motion of his walk, rocking him.

'I'm here,' she said, shedding her coat and bag and reaching for Kit.

'I think he's hungry,' Ben said, 'and I didn't want to offer him a bottle, not when the feeding's going so well. Shall I put the kettle on?'

Liv flashed him a grateful smile. 'Thanks. You're a star. Hi, Missy. Are you all right, darling?'

Missy nodded from her high chair up against the kitchen table and blew Liv a kiss. 'Missy dough,' she said, holding up a handful of sticky pink gloop and grinning.

'Play-dough,' Ben explained. 'My sisters make it.

I rang Janie and asked her for the recipe. It's revolting—flour, salt and oil in about equal quantities. Disgusting. Oh, and cream of tartar for some reason, and food colouring, of course. It tastes quite vile—there's no danger she'll eat it.'

'I'm glad about that. Is it lovely, darling?' she asked her daughter, and was treated to a huge grin.

'Missy help,' she told her proudly.

Ben gave a crooked grin. 'Missy stirred it with me while it was cold. She was firmly out of the way while I was heating it.'

Liv was relieved to hear it. She curled up in the chair to feed Kit, and Missy squashed and pressed and pulled off lumps and rolled them in her sticky little hands, and Ben helped her cut out shapes with a biscuit cutter until the kettle boiled, then he made some tea and set it down beside Liv.

'Here. You look as if you could do with it. How did you get on?'

'Brilliant,' she said, flashing him a smile. 'The nearly-new shop had a lovely dress—it's in that bag. You couldn't be a love and hang it up, could you? I just dropped it because of the baby and I'd hate it to get creased.'

He frowned as he pulled the dress out.

'What?' she asked sharply, suddenly worried by his disapproval. 'What's wrong with it?'

'Your insecurities are showing,' he told her gently. 'There's nothing wrong with it. It's a lovely dress. I just—'

'What? You disapprove?'

'I wish I'd known. I didn't realise you'd gone to town for this; I thought you might have a dress in your wardrobe. I would have bought you one, Liv—a new one. I offered you the money last night.'

She felt hot colour sting her cheeks. 'I didn't want you to buy me one, Ben. I need to be independent, and it's hardly worn. Besides, it was all I could afford. Don't be so stuffy. I always used to haunt the second-hand shops and charity shops—and anyway, it's not exactly a chain-store rag. At least this one's a decent make.'

'There's nothing wrong with the dress. I just hate the thought of you having to do that, after all you had. I wish you'd let me treat you.'

'No.' Her voice was firm, perhaps a little harsh, but she really didn't want him 'treating' her. Masquerading as his housekeeper felt enough like charity, without taking any more, and she was far from being his 'kept woman', with all the perks that might entitle her to.

She tried again to explain. 'I need to be independent, Ben. I have to do it. Oscar sponged on me—I can't let myself do it to anyone else. I know how it feels to be on the other side. Besides, it's only a damn dress. So it's second-hand. That means it's been worn. So has everything else I own. Just because it was someone else's body in it doesn't make it so very different, does it?'

'Oh, Liv.' He reached over and ruffled her hair, just gently. 'Don't get crabby with me. I'm just feeling guilty because I asked you to the party. It was my idea. You can't afford to buy dresses, and it's a business do, anyway. I could have taken it out of petty cash or something.'

Her ruffled feathers subsided—a bit. 'It's all right.

It feels better this way,' she told him firmly, and he dropped the subject.

Still, all the time she was getting ready to go out, she was conscious of a nagging disappointment that he couldn't have just said it was a nice dress and left it at that. She wished they hadn't had to have the conversation—that she'd pretended she'd had the dress or something.

Anything rather than cause a rift between them.

She put the dress on without even looking at it, fastened her strappy shoes and went to check on the children. They were both asleep, and she'd fed Kit just half an hour ago. With any luck he'd sleep through till they got back, and if not, Mrs Greer had instructions to give him a little bottle to settle him again.

She was here—Liv could hear her talking to Ben in the kitchen—and her presence gave her the courage to face him. She put on her coat, buttoned to the neck, picked up her bag and made her way down to the hall, just as Ben emerged from the kitchen.

'Ah, Liv, you're ready. Well done. Shall we go, or do you want to give Mrs Greer any last-minute instructions?'

'How well you know me,' she said with a smile, and went and spoke to her. You're stalling, she told herself when she finally ran out of idiotic instructions, and went back to Ben.

'All set,' she told him, and he ushered her out to the waiting car. They were at the hotel in minutes, and he parked the car, opened her door for her and escorted her in.

'Want to leave your coat?' he asked, and she slipped it off her shoulders and handed it to him to give to the cloakroom attendant. Then he turned back to her, ran a critical eye over her and smiled.

'It's stunning,' he said softly. 'You look absolutely gorgeous.'

And suddenly, because of his words and the approval in his eyes and the warmth of his smile, she *felt* gorgeous.

Truly, radiantly beautiful for the first time in years—and she was with a man who would never be more than her best and dearest friend...

CHAPTER FOUR

IT WAS a party like thousands she'd been to before, where most of the people knew each other by sight, and so people circulated easily, slipping seamlessly in and out of groups and swapping trivia and little snippets of gossip.

Liv didn't know anyone, of course, as all of them were totally out of her circle, but Ben attached her firmly to his arm and led her amongst the crowd, introducing her as 'my friend Liv'. She noticed a few women looking at her sideways, possibly trying to work out if she really *could* be Liv Kensington or not, but for the most part people smiled and said hello and carried on chatting.

And Ben, of course, was charm personified. He smiled and laughed easily, and remembered everyone's names, and Liv was impressed. There was a bit of networking, the odd conversation tinged with business talk, but Ben's line was logistics and Liv had never really understood what exactly logistics meant, apart from the fact that it was some sort of coordinated haulage and delivery system.

She did her social smile bit until her cheeks ached, then she excused herself and slipped out to the Ladies' for a moment of peace and quiet.

She went into one of the cubicles, and a moment later heard two women come in, talking in conspiratorial tones. 'Did you see that woman with Ben

Warriner?' one said. 'He called her Liv—I'm sure it's Liv Kensington, the model.'

'It can't be—she was scrawny, and this woman certainly isn't scrawny!'

Liv looked down at her stomach and sighed silently. The conversation carried on.

'But her face looks so familiar. I reckon it must be—I wonder what the story is?'

'I heard she's staying with him,' the second woman murmured. 'Interesting.'

The first woman laughed. 'Absolutely, but Tash won't be thrilled.'

Liv froze. Tash? Who was Tash? He'd told her there wasn't anyone. Had he been lying, to make her feel better? Or maybe she was an old lover, in the throes of unrequited lust.

Whatever, Liv didn't think her presence was interfering in the love of a lifetime. If there had been anyone serious, surely Ben would have talked about her and introduced her? And he certainly hadn't.

Someone else came in and the women dropped the conversation. Liv waited while doors opened and shut, loos flushed and hand-dryers roared, and finally, when it had all gone quiet again, she felt safe to come out.

Not that she'd done anything that necessitated her lurking, but she didn't want an embarrassing confrontation. She went back into the function room where the party was being held, and saw Ben standing on the other side of the room, in the company of a beautiful blonde.

The mysterious Tash? Possibly. Tall, reed-thin, elegant, she swayed towards him, her tinkling laughter reaching Liv across the room and grating on her nerves. She laid a possessive hand on his cheek, and he smiled and turned his face into her hand, kissing it.

A jolt of desire shot through Liv, shocking her, and for the first time she saw Ben, her old friend and confidant, as a man—a real, hot-blooded, passionate man of the world. A man who would take a woman in his arms and love her till the moon faded to a distant sliver of white in the morning mist, and the sun touched the horizon with fingers of gold.

A real man.

Liv felt the shock of recognition down to her toes, and with it came an unfamiliar feeling, one she couldn't understand. Then suddenly Ben looked up, over the woman's hand, and met her eyes. He straightened, smiled at the woman and removed her hand from his cheek with a curiously gentle gesture.

Then he was striding towards Liv, wrapping a possessive hand around her elbow and smiling down at her. 'Rescue me,' he said under his breath, and she fell into step beside him as they headed for the dance floor.

'Who from?' she asked, still reeling from the shock of her sudden awareness of him. She could feel the imprint of every finger on her arm, the heat of his body radiating through her as he led her towards the middle of the floor.

'Tash—Natasha Barker. Old flame—thinks she still owns me. It was never anything serious but she won't give up. Every time I see her she tries again, and it just messes her up.'

'You might try being less flirtatious with her,' Liv said, finally working out that the strange feeling she'd had when he'd kissed the woman's hand was jealousy. How odd. She'd never felt jealous before, and she'd often seen him with women.

Just never, perhaps, with all that masculine charm in action, as it had been with the beautiful and unrequited Tash. It was the tender way he'd kissed her hand, the smile in his eyes, the way he focused on her as if she'd been the centre of his world.

The way he was focusing on Liv now.

He turned her into his arms, laid his outspread hand against her waist and drew her gently towards him. She rested her hand on his shoulder, feeling for the first time the sheer power of the muscle under the fine wool cloth. Her other hand lay in his, utterly aware of the breadth of his palm, the warm, dry fingers curled loosely round hers, the slight pressure of his thumb tracing idly against her knuckles.

He was taller than her, tall enough that even in her heels she had to tip her head to meet his eyes. They were shadowed by the subtle lighting, mysterious, their expression unreadable. His mouth, so close, was firm and full and infinitely kissable. She desperately wanted to taste it, to taste him, to feel the touch of his lips on hers again to see if it had been a fluke.

His hand eased her nearer, and she rested her head on his shoulder and swayed with him to the music as she had done so many times before. This time, though, something was different.

This time she knew he was more than a friend. She knew without doubt why she'd run to him, when the world was going to pieces around her and Oscar had thrown them out.

She loved him, and from that moment on, nothing between them could ever be quite the same again.

* * *

It was the longest two hours of her life. She had to smile and laugh and look intelligent, and all she wanted to do was run away into a dark corner and hide until she'd come to terms with her feelings.

Finally Ben looked at her searchingly and glanced at his watch. 'We've been here long enough for me to do my duty—we can go, if you like,' he murmured. 'Want to sneak home?'

She nodded, suddenly unable to pretend to enjoy herself any longer. 'Please. I expect Kit's screaming.'

He chuckled and ushered her towards the foyer, looking much more like his old familiar self than the suave, sexy stranger he'd been just an hour ago when she'd seen him talking to Tash.

And dancing with her. She'd danced with that stranger, had understood for the first time what Kate meant about all that testosterone, and wondered how she could have been so slow, so inexplicably dense, that it had taken her ten years to realise that she was attracted to him.

Not just attracted. The magnet that drew her to him was love, deep as the sea and utterly irrevocable. The only problem was, it was totally one-sided. Ben didn't even notice her except as the girl next door who'd grown into a beautiful woman and still been his little Liv. He was protective of her, mildly amused and often aggravated by her crazy behaviour, tolerant of her nonsense, he shared her sense of humour—and if she'd had two heads he probably wouldn't have noticed.

She was just Liv—treasured, cared for but never loved, never cherished, never wanted as a woman.

Just now, she thought, that probably suited her. She was still raw from her relationship with Oscar, and she wasn't ready for another relationship. But when she was, what then?

Loving Ben as she clearly did, how could she live a lie with another man?

A deep sigh issued from her chest, and Ben shot her a curious look. 'You OK, Liv?'

'Fine. Just tired.'

'Not long now.' He retrieved their coats, ushered her into the car and whisked her home in no time, and they went inside to blissful silence broken only by the low murmur of the television.

Mrs Greer was in the kitchen, watching the end of a chat show, and there was no sound from the children.

'Not heard a peep,' she told them. 'I've checked on them a couple of times, but they've both been out for the count, bless their hearts. They're lovely little mites.'

She stood up, turning off the television, and Ben glanced at Liv.

'I'll run Mrs Greer home—fancy making some coffee?'

She shook her head. 'I think, if you don't mind, I'll go on up. I'm tired, and Kit's bound to wake soon. Thank you, Mrs Greer. What do I owe you?'

'Oh, nothing, my dear. It's all settled—Ben's paid me already. I hope you had a lovely time.'

She dredged up a smile, wondering if she should tackle Ben about the babysitting money or just let it go. After all, it wasn't a patch on the cost of the dress he'd wanted to buy. 'I did—thank you,' she answered almost mechanically. 'It was wonderful.'

It wasn't entirely a lie, she thought as she trudged up the stairs to her lonely bed. Dancing with Ben had been wonderful in a rather masochistic way. It was her feelings that were difficult to deal with, and they weren't going to get any easier, she realised, as time went by.

Perhaps this wasn't going to work. Perhaps it was time to go, time to move on and find somewhere proper to live. Oscar would have to support them, and she would just have to eat her pride and insist that he meet his responsibilities, unless she could find another such job somewhere else.

'Don't be stupid,' she told herself tiredly. 'You can hardly cope with Ben, never mind a family—and who else would put up with Kit screaming and Missy's toys and her chaotic disorganisation?

'Nobody,' she said to the empty hall. 'And Oscar will leave the country before he'll give you a brass farthing. You're stuck here, Olivia. Just make the best of it.'

At the top of the stairs, she hesitated for a moment and then walked down the landing, pausing for a moment in the doorway of his bedroom. It was a lovely room, running over the kitchen from front to back of the house, with a big window at each end and a lavishly fitted bathroom off it.

The furnishings were simple and mostly white— the big bed, set in the middle of the long wall, was made up with a sumptuous down quilt and pillows in plain white linen, covered with a heavy cotton bedspread in a textured design with a thick, weighty fringe. A bank of fitted wardrobes, an easy chair with a table and a reading light, all in pale limed wood, a cosy rug along the floor at the foot of the bed and a few large and striking pictures on the walls made up the rest of the furnishings.

Usually the room was tidy, but tonight there was evidence of his quick change. His clothes were dropped where he'd taken them off, a pair of trousers straggling off the edge of the neatly made bed, a shirt dangling from the chair where he'd abandoned it. She remembered that he'd been waiting for a phone call and had showered and changed in record time after the call.

She picked up the trousers and folded them neatly, and bundled the shirt into her arms to drop into the laundry basket. On impulse she buried her nose in the shirt, drawing in the masculine scent of him, the warm, musky aroma that was Ben.

The bed drew her eyes, and she wondered how much time he'd spent in there with Tash, or any of the other beautiful women who had been at the party that night.

'It's none of your damn business,' she said crossly, crushing the jealous rage that rose in her. 'Forget it. He's not yours to want.'

She dumped the shirt ruthlessly in the laundry basket on the way past, and went in to check on the children. Kit was beginning to fidget, sucking his fists, fussing and fretting. She lifted him before he could wake Missy and carried him through to her room to feed him.

Her dress was a bit impractical for breastfeeding, she thought with a wry smile, and, putting Kit down on the bed, she undid the side zip and wriggled out of it. She hunted for her dressing gown, but couldn't find it, and Kit was starting to fuss, so she climbed on the bed, sat cross-legged at the top and took off her bra to feed him.

That was how Ben found her a few minutes later,

when he tapped on the door and walked in without
waiting for her to answer.

'Sorry,' he said hastily, and backed out, and she
closed her eyes and let out a shaky sigh. Damn.

'Hang on,' she called, and pulled her nightshirt on
over her head, giving herself a modicum of cover.
'Come back.'

He opened the door cautiously and came in. 'Sorry
to barge in,' he said ruefully. 'I knew you'd be feeding him. I didn't realise you were undressed.'

'I had to take the dress off—no way into the front
of it and he was getting impatient,' she said with a
wry grin. 'I didn't mean to scandalise you. Did you
want something?'

He shook his head and perched on the end of the
bed, staring out of the window over the midnight garden. 'I'm making coffee. I wondered if you wanted
any, or if you'd rather have tea, or if you don't want
either.'

'Tea would be lovely, actually,' she said guiltily.
He seemed to spend his life making her tea. 'I'll come
down.'

'No, stay there, I'll bring it to you,' he insisted, and
went out, closing the door softly.

She put her head back against the headboard and
sighed deeply. If he were her lover, she thought wistfully, he'd sit closer, look down at the baby feeding,
stroke his cheek, perhaps, with a gentle finger.

Then, when she'd finished feeding him, he'd take
the baby from her and lay him down in his cot, then
join her on the bed and make long, slow, lazy love
to her.

'You're mad,' she said crossly, sitting up and wrig-
gling into a more comfortable position. 'Two hours

ago he was just Ben, your best friend. Now you're having fantasies about him kissing you and touching you and—' She broke off, biting her lip.

She couldn't stay here with him, not like this. She'd be driven mad by her own emotions.

However, she had no choice. There was nowhere else for her to go, nowhere to take the children safely at the beginning of the winter when she had no money and no hope of earning any.

There was no realistic possibility of going back to Oscar or asking him for money, either—not that she wanted to, but she had to think of the children.

At least here they were all safe and warm and fed. She'd just have to stifle her feelings, pretend they didn't exist, put them away.

There was a tap on the door, and it opened a crack. 'Room service,' he said softly, and she smiled despite herself.

'Come in, Ben. I've finished feeding him, anyway. He's asleep.'

He put two mugs down on the bedside table and reached out for Kit. 'I'll cuddle him—you drink your tea,' he instructed, and propped the baby up against his broad shoulder.

What was it about big men with tiny babies that made her go all gooey? She drank her tea slowly, watching him interacting with the little one, and her gut clenched when he pressed his lips to the baby's forehead and kissed him gently.

'He's out for the count—want me to do his nappy and put him down for you?' he murmured.

She scrambled off the bed and took him, dumping her mug on the way. 'I'll do it. You drink your tea.'

She had him tucked up in moments, and looked up

from the crib to find Ben standing in the doorway, silently watching her. 'You're good with them,' he said quietly.

'So are you—you ought to have some.'

He gave a soft, derisive snort and turned away. 'Not much danger of that,' he said, or something like it. She wasn't quite sure. He hadn't really said it to her, anyway, so there was no point in asking him to repeat it.

She followed him down the corridor, then hesitated when she realised he was going into his room. He turned back, his eyes brooding.

'Are you all right?' he asked.

She nodded. 'Thanks for taking me to the party.'

His laugh was gentle. 'You hated it.'

'Not all of it,' she said truthfully, and added silently, for her ears alone, Not the dancing. I definitely didn't hate the dancing.

'I'll see you tomorrow,' he said, and closed the door with a soft click. For a moment she stood there, longing to follow him, and then with a heavy sigh she turned back to her own room, closed the door and slid into bed alone.

'Get used to it,' she told herself firmly. 'This is how it is.'

She woke in the night to a brilliant idea. She could go back to modelling. Not her figure, of course, but her face. Maybe even her figure, if she could persuade herself to stop eating so much and work out a bit.

Ben had a weights room next to the utility room, filled with all sorts of equipment. If she went in there every day while the children were asleep and worked out on the treadmill or something, she might get firmed up enough to do *some* modelling work, even if not on the scale she had before.

And then, of course, she'd have money, and be able to support herself and the children without being a burden on Ben.

Brilliant. She'd contact her old agent in the morning—or on Monday morning, in fact, as tomorrow was Sunday. She'd be able to tell her what the chances were.

With a glimmer of hope on the horizon for the first time in weeks, she snuggled down under the quilt, closed her eyes again and went back to sleep.

'Rise and shine!'

She dragged her head out from under the pillow and rolled over, blinking blearily at him.

'What time is it?'

'Eight-thirty—Kit's hungry, Missy's demanding breakfast and I thought you might want to know. Here's a cup of tea—I'll fetch you the baby and take Missy down with me.'

She struggled into a sitting position and looked around. Daylight leaked in round the curtain, and in the gloom she could see a mug on the bedside table. She latched on to it like a drowning man with a straw, and no sooner had she taken the first glorious, scalding sip than Ben reappeared with Kit squalling noisily in his arms.

'One baby,' he said with a grin, and headed for the door with Missy in tow.

'Missy b'ekfast,' Missy said cheerfully as she followed him. 'Missy want egg.'

'Say please.'

'P'ease.'

'Good girl.'

Their voices drifted out of range, and Liv smiled and leant back against the pillows and fed the baby, leaning sideways so she could sip her tea without any danger of scalding him.

She was beginning to feel disgustingly self-satisfied about her ability to feed him. He never needed top-ups now, and he was much more contented. She felt positively smug as she put him down, climbed out of bed and wandered through to the nursery to change him before putting him down again.

She found Ben in the kitchen with Missy, eating scrambled egg.

'Where's mine?' she asked with mock indignation, and he grinned.

'Keeping fresh. I'll make it in a tick. You could pour the coffee.'

She slid his across the table towards him and sat down, one leg hitched up on the chair underneath her. Missy was paddling her spoon in the scrambled egg and getting it everywhere, but Ben didn't seem to care.

Oscar, she thought idly, would have had a fit and demanded she feed the child. Ben was happy to let her play.

'I thought I'd contact my old agent—ask about doing some more modelling,' she said out of the blue.

Ben went still, then carried on forking egg into his mouth. 'Why?'

She shrugged. 'Money—what else? I have to live and support the children, and you don't want me here. Let's face it, Ben, I'm a lousy housekeeper. I spend all my time up to my eyes in the children and get nothing done, and Mrs Greer spends all *her* time clearing up after us, and it's not exactly fair on you.'

'It'll get better.'

She sighed and raked a hand through her hair, tousling the tangled strands hopelessly. 'No, Ben, it won't. It's not fair on you.'

'Why don't you let me be the judge of that?' he asked quietly.

She sighed and sipped her coffee, then tried again. 'You had a life before we arrived.'

'Yes—a lonely, empty life with nothing in it but work. I like having you here, Liv. Believe me.'

'You are sweet to us.'

He made a disgusted noise, and she smiled sadly. 'You are. Don't be macho and funny about it. You've been really kind, Ben, and it's not right to take advantage any more.'

'You're not taking advantage.'

'Yes, we are.'

'No. OK, I'll admit as a housekeeper you aren't able to give it your best shot because of the kids, but there are other ways in which you more than earn your keep. Just having someone to come home to— someone who knows me, who can understand my sense of humour, knows my likes and dislikes, won't let me sulk and grump—someone who smiles and says, "How was your day?" when I come in.'

'That's not a housekeeper, Ben—that's a wife,' she said wistfully.

He looked up, his eyes unreadable. 'So marry me.'

Very carefully, without spilling a drop, she put her coffee down. Her heart was pounding, her hopes piling up so high she thought she'd suffocate on them. 'What?'

'Marry me,' he repeated. 'Be there for me when I come home, and I'll be there for you when the children are sick or things go wrong.'

'Why on earth would you want to marry me?' she asked, hardly daring to hope.

A wry grin flickered over his face. 'Because I love you?' he said easily.

For a moment she almost believed him, then hope took second place to common sense, and she gave a short laugh.

'You're such a sweetheart,' she said kindly. 'I don't know what I would have done without you the last few weeks, but don't you think this is going a little too far?'

He shook his head. 'No. It's a crazy idea, I know, but why not? What else is there for us? Oscar doesn't want you, there's nobody in my life—I'm not talking about a permanent solution, necessarily, Liv—just something to tide you over until you know what you want—something to protect you and give you security, give the children security.'

She sat back and stared at him. 'You really mean it, don't you?' she said, stunned. 'You really are asking me to marry you.'

He nodded. 'Apparently so. I hadn't planned it, it just came out, but the more I think about it, the better I like it. So, what do you say, Liv? Will you marry me? Let me look after you and keep you safe?'

She ruthlessly crushed the impulse to say yes.

'Why?' she said instead. 'What's in it for you, Ben? What's the catch?'

He shrugged easily and leant back in the chair, one hand idly toying with his mug. 'No catch. You get security and a meal ticket and an allowance, I get a ready-made family to call my own and come home to. Strikes me I'm definitely getting the best part of the bargain.'

He really was serious. A thought occurred to her, and warm colour crept up over her cheeks. 'Um— what about—you know—?'

'I'm not a monster, Liv,' he said softly. 'I know we don't have that kind of a relationship. Nothing would change. You'll stay in your room, I'll stay in mine, and if you find anyone you love and want to marry, I'll let you go.'

'And you?' she said softly. 'What about if you find someone you love?'

He met her eyes, and his own were immeasurably sad. 'It won't happen, Liv. Love like that happens only once in a lifetime, and it won't happen to me again.'

She dragged in a deep breath and looked away, unable to bear the pain in his eyes another moment. Who? When? Why hadn't he told her?

'Think about it,' he said. 'I'm going to get dressed and go for a run, then I thought we might go to Aldeburgh later and get those fish and chips I promised you. All right?'

She nodded, and he went out, leaving her there feeling shell-shocked. Could she do it? Marry him, without any mention of love between them? Share his life and not his bed, long for him, yearn for the feel of his arms around her and yet know it would never be?

But what was the alternative? To leave him, uproot them all and go into some ghastly rented house and struggle alone without his friendship and company? And why? Just because she couldn't have it all?

Just to be near him, to share his life even in such a platonic way was more than she could have dreamed of, and if he felt the dubious benefit of her company compensated him for the chaos the children would bring into his life, who was she to complain?

And the children would benefit hugely from his influence and the love he would undoubtedly shower on them.

He was right, she realised. He was lonely, and so was she, and if she married him they would both at least be content. She would never love anyone else, and someone had obviously stolen his heart and left it in tatters.

Neither of them was destined to find happiness elsewhere, it seemed, so why not find peace and contentment with each other? There was a lot to be said for it, and it knocked spots off the stormy and unsatisfactory relationship she'd had with Oscar.

And maybe one day, when she got her figure back and had stopped breastfeeding, maybe then he might notice that she was a woman, as well as a friend.

Maybe then they could have a real marriage, and she would know the touch of his lips and the feel of his arms around her in the quiet of the night.

Thoughtful, she bathed herself and Missy and dressed them both for a winter walk by the sea, and then bathed Kit and changed him into a snuggly suit.

She heard Ben's bedroom door open, and he came out on to the landing just as she emerged from the children's room. He was dressed in jeans and a thick sweatshirt, his hair still damp from the shower, and he looked good enough to eat.

'Yes,' she said impulsively.

He looked at her, puzzled, his brow pleating. 'What?'

'I said yes, I'll marry you.'

Something flickered in his eyes, then he smiled ruefully and held out his hands.

'Good. Come here.'

He drew her into his arms, lowered his mouth and kissed her—just once, just lightly, but it was enough to blow away the cobwebs of delusion and make her wonder if she'd just made the biggest mistake of her life...

CHAPTER FIVE

THEY had a wonderful day. Kit managed to sleep in all the right places, Missy was delicious and Ben—well, Ben was just Ben, funny, tolerant and thoughtful.

They ate fish and chips on the sea wall, with Kit asleep behind them in the buggy and Missy snuggled up between them being finger-fed little slivers of carefully boned fish by Liv, while she clutched one of Ben's chips in her sticky little hand and sucked it periodically.

Liv revelled in the greasy, sticky meal. 'I could so easily be enormous,' she said with satisfaction, licking her fingers, and Ben chuckled.

'No, you couldn't. You're just hungry because you're feeding the baby and recovering from pregnancy, and you're on the go all the time.'

She wished it was true. She had a horrible feeling, though, that her days of eating only three tomatoes and a low-fat yoghurt all day were long gone. She'd have to tackle his fitness room and see if she couldn't work off a few of the surplus pounds and inches.

But not now. Now, she was sitting on the sea wall next to Ben, with Missy sucking on her mangled chip, and the sun was out and the sea was calm and it was a beautiful mild day, and she intended to enjoy it.

Ben pointed out the lifeboat station, and they strolled along and looked at the lifeboat, Ben taking

Missy round the boathouse display area while Liv stayed with Kit at the bottom of the stairs.

Then they walked along the front and saw a tiny little house in the middle of the road, and she thought it looked like a doll's house. 'It's too small to live in,' she said doubtfully, eyeing the miniature dwelling, but Ben shook his head.

'I think it's a holiday cottage. Certainly people do stay in it from time to time, if not always. There are several odd holiday cottages round here, like the House in the Clouds, which is a converted water tower. It's up the coast—I'll show you one day. It's amazing.'

'Missy buggy,' Missy demanded, and Liv stopped the buggy and put her daughter in next to Kit, and strapped her in, removing the soggy remains of the chip and wiping her hand.

'Want dink,' she announced, and Ben glanced across at Liv.

'Sounds like a fine idea. How about finding a café somewhere?' he suggested, and so they went back to the car and drove up the coast until they found a little tea room.

The timing was perfect. Kit woke up ready for a feed, so Liv sat in the corner with her coat draped artfully over her shoulders and fed him discreetly while Ben poured the tea and helped Missy with her juice.

It all felt so easy, so natural, that they could have been married for years.

Maybe it will work, she thought in amazement. Maybe it's not such a silly idea after all. If I can just keep my feelings under wraps—how can it hurt if I love him? It just means everything I do for him will be for love and not out of duty. That will surely just make it easier.

'Shall we go back?' he suggested.

She nodded. Kit was back in the buggy asleep, she'd finished her second cup of tea and there was no reason to stay, other than that she had enjoyed playing happy families with him, but she could do that at home for the rest of her life, she realised in slight wonderment.

'About the wedding,' she said suddenly as they set off in the car, and he looked at her keenly, his expression inscrutable.

'What about it? Are you having second thoughts?'

She laughed softly. 'No, not at all—unless you are?'

He shook his head. 'No. The more I think about it, the better I like the idea.'

'Ditto.' They shared a smile, and she went on, 'I just wondered when you had in mind?'

He shrugged. 'Whenever. I haven't had time to think about it. What do you want to do?'

She looked down at her lap, playing thoughtfully with a fold in her coat. 'I thought—it might be nice to be married before Christmas.'

His hand came out and covered hers, squeezing gently. 'I agree. Let's go home, look at my diary and set a date, shall we? And, Liv—I don't think anyone else needs to know why we're doing this, do they?'

She thought of her parents, living in the Algarve at the moment, who would be delighted if a little puzzled when she married Ben. Explaining to them would be next to impossible. His parents, likewise, would give them the third degree if they had the slightest clue, and his sisters Janie and Clare would be like a couple of terriers on a rat.

No, they would all have to think it was a love match—which of course, from Liv's point of view, it was. At least she'd be able to look them all in the eye and say she'd loved Ben for years!

'No, they don't,' she agreed. 'It will be much easier if we just tell them we've been a bit slow on the uptake.' And, of course, utterly truthful. One thing she found quite impossible was lying to anyone. To tell her family the truth would be much easier—even if it was a one-sided and edited version.

The diary came up with a few possible dates, the first being the following week.

'We do need to let everyone know and give them a chance to get here,' she said slowly. 'Unless, of course, you planned just to do it and tell them afterwards?'

Was it that funny? Whatever, he threw back his head and laughed so hard he nearly choked. 'With my sisters?' he said when he drew breath. 'I don't think so. My life would be hell for the next several hundred years. They'll be here, and my parents, and your parents will want to come over from Portugal, I imagine?'

She nodded. 'Why don't we ask them all and see if we can come up with a consensus on the date?'

So they did. They spent the rest of Sunday afternoon on the phone to various of their relations telling them the news, and Liv listened to Ben's glib lies and wished they were true. At least when she said she loved him, she truly meant it.

Her parents were ecstatic. 'Darling, I've never said this before,' her mother told her passionately, 'but I

always hated Oscar, and to think of you married to
Ben is just wonderful! I've always looked at the two
of you together and wondered when you'd realise,
and I'm so glad you've finally come to your senses!'

Liv looked at the phone in amazement. Her mother
knew? Why hadn't she said anything? Not that it
would have helped, not until now, not until they'd
reached this point in their lives.

'So, when can you come over?' she asked, dragging her mother back from eulogising over Ben to the
subject of the wedding date.

'Whenever you like. We're totally free—well,
we're not, but there's nothing so important we can't
cancel it for your wedding, darling! I just can't get
over the fact that you left Oscar and didn't tell us, but
of course you've been with Ben, so I expect you've
been too busy to think about us, you sly little thing!'

Liv flushed guiltily. She had meant to tell her parents, but she hadn't known quite how to put it without
worrying them out of their minds, and they'd retired
to the Algarve young because of her father's ill
health. She didn't want to put any unnecessary worry
on them, and they didn't have enough money to support her, which of course they would have offered to
do.

'So shall we liaise with all the others and come
back to you?' she suggested.

'Good idea—but give me plenty of warning. Do
you want me to come over and help plan it? Where
will you get married from? Not London, surely?
Woodbridge? What about flowers for the church?'

'Mum, stop it,' Liv interrupted gently. 'We'll arrange the wedding. It's only going to be simple, probably in the register office.'

'Olivia, no!' her mother protested. 'You *must* have a church wedding, darling!'

'We'll see,' she compromised.

'That means no,' her mother said flatly, having had years of practice with the expression.

'No, it means I'll talk to Ben. I'll come back to you, Mum, as soon as I know anything. All right?'

She placed the receiver in its cradle and turned to Ben. 'She wants us to have a church wedding.'

'So do I,' he said quietly.

She thought about it for a second, and nodded. 'I do, too, really. I just thought you wouldn't, as it's not—'

She broke off, and he looked searchingly at her. 'Not what, Liv?'

She shrugged. 'Not a real marriage.'

'Yes, it is,' he corrected, his voice soft and a little gruff. 'It's about sharing and commitment and being there for each other, smoothing out life's little inequalities. It's about kindness and tolerance and giving the children a decent foundation for their lives. It's about friendship and give and take and all sorts of other things too numerous to mention that are vastly more important than a transient passion.'

She coloured, thinking of the way she'd felt in his arms when they'd danced, and how very much she wanted that last, extra element of their relationship.

'I suppose you're right,' she agreed quietly. 'So what do we do now?'

'We could go to church? They have evensong—we could go and talk to the vicar and discuss it with him—he might be able to give us possible dates. It doesn't have to be on a Saturday, does it?'

She shook her head. 'No, I don't suppose it does. What about the children? Can we take them?'

'We'll get Mrs Greer.'

'Poor woman. She must be sick of us. What about her husband?'

'He's an invalid. They need all the money they can get. Anyway, she likes to get out. She feels a bit trapped with him sometimes.'

So he rang Mrs Greer, and she agreed to come round and look after the children, and Liv looked in her wardrobe and finally came up with a wrapover skirt that she'd worn after Missy was born and a nice jumper, under her long coat that covered a multitude of sins.

The service was lovely, a choral evensong that was very simple and moving, and she looked around the church and thought, Yes, I want to be married here. I want to make my vows to Ben in a place like this, where thousands of other couples have made the same vows in front of God. I wonder how many of them stayed together? Tragically few, she thought, and vowed that she would be there for Ben come hell or high water, no matter what happened to them, until such time as he wanted to walk away.

And then, because she loved him, she'd let him go.

'Come on, let's go and talk to him.'

She looked up, startled, to find that the service was over and the congregation were moving towards the door, chatting easily to each other and smiling at the young strangers in their midst.

The vicar was delighted to welcome them, and when Ben explained that they wanted to get married, he delved into the folds of his cassock and pulled out a slim diary. 'How about coming to see me—or shall I come to you?'

'Could you?' Ben suggested. 'It would make it easier for Liv because of the babies.'

'Babies?' he echoed. 'So have you been married before?'

Liv shook her head. 'No.'

'So are they yours?' he asked Ben, and Ben shook his head.

'No, not mine. Not yet. I wish they were,' he added softly, and his arm came round Liv and gave her a hug. All part of the act, she thought, and slid her arm round his waist. It looked good, and it was a perfect excuse to touch him. She didn't get many, and she wasn't going to waste this one!

'Sounds like you two have quite a story to tell,' the vicar said gently, and smiled at them. 'How about ten tomorrow?'

'Fine.' Ben dictated the address, gave him directions and that was that.

The vicar held out his hand, and Liv had to remove her arm from round Ben's waist to shake it, and after that there was no real excuse to put it back, so she didn't. She just wished that she had the right to, that their marriage would be more real in the physical sense, and that she had the right of a wife to touch and hold and caress her loved one.

She blinked back tears and followed Ben out to the car, and sat in silence for a moment.

'Lovely church,' Ben said quietly.

'Yes, it is. Beautiful.'

'Are you going to be all right with this, Liv?'

What did he mean? Did he realise how she felt? 'Of course,' she told him firmly. 'Why not?'

He shrugged. 'Well, I'm not Oscar.'

'Thank God.'

'You loved him once.'

'I thought I did. What about you? You haven't told me about the woman who broke your heart.'

He started the engine, his mouth a grim line. 'No. Don't worry about me, Liv. As long as you're OK with this marriage, that's all I'm concerned about.'

He didn't say any more on the way home, and when they got back he turned the car round, left the engine running and took Mrs Greer home while Liv started to prepare supper. Kit was gurgling happily in the bouncing cradle, Missy was busy with a stacking toy and she was getting married.

What more could she ask for?

Ben's love, her heart replied, and she shut her eyes and plumbed deep down inside herself for the strength to go through with this, to give it all she could.

And maybe one day his broken heart would ease and he would see her as a woman...

The wedding was planned for the last Friday in November, less than two weeks away. The Saturday was already booked, and nearer to Christmas it became chaotic with various carol services, more weddings and christenings and so on. On Monday afternoon they arranged a special licence, booked the caterers and drew up a guest list.

By Tuesday morning, all she had to do was choose a dress. Ben had insisted that he would pay for it. 'All you have to do is find it and have it put on one side, and I'll pay for it and collect it. And please, Liv, don't argue with me this time.'

She didn't. It was her wedding day, and she wanted

to wear a beautiful dress for it, not only for herself
but for Ben. The trouble was, no matter how beautiful
the dress, it had to go on her body.

She stood in front of the mirror in her underwear
and sighed. Where had her figure gone? She used to
have endless legs and jutting hipbones and collar-
bones like coathangers, and things would drape on her
and look elegant.

Now she had bulges. Not curves. Bulges.

Her bust bulged—boy, did it bulge! Especially just
before she fed Kit. And her waist was shot away, that
hand-span slenderness gone for ever. Below her
tummy-button was a little blimp, a firm little bulge
that no amount of exercise seemed to get rid of.

She knew that. She'd been trying sit-ups and en-
ergetic housework, and nothing seemed to make a
scrap of difference. She'd have a go in Ben's gym,
but she didn't expect it to work.

She supposed that once your abdomen had been all
the way out there, it wasn't so easy to drag it all back
into the tiny space it had once occupied. And then
there were the legs. They were still long—not even
pregnancy could change that—but the three-inch gap
between her thighs at the top seemed to have vanished
completely.

She'd been a size eight—tiny for someone of five
foot eight—and now she was a size twelve, and her
bust was pushing a fourteen.

There was a knock on the door. 'Liv? It's Kate—
Ben said to come up. Can I come in?'

She considered hiding in her dressing gown, and
thought better of it. 'Yes, come in. Help me—I'm
staring at my body and hating it.'

Kate closed the door behind her, eyed Liv critically

up and down and laughed. 'You hate your body? Try
mine for a few days. I'm three inches shorter than
you, I probably weigh a stone more—you have no
problems, believe me.'

Liv smiled at her old friend in the mirror. 'You
weren't a model. You don't have all the world looking at you and thinking, Gosh, Liv Kensington's getting fat!'

'Nor do you,' Kate said bluntly, dropping on to the
bed and tucking her legs up underneath her. 'All the
world is looking at whoever it is now and thinking, I
hate the cow, she's so skinny! Trust me, Liv, nobody's looking at you any longer, and even if they
were, you look gorgeous.'

Liv didn't believe her, but she did feel a bit better
knowing that the focus of attention had moved on.
Nobody cared about her any more. It didn't matter if
she had lost her figure, and she had two beautiful
children to show for it.

'You're a dear girl,' she said with affection, and
pulled on her jeans and jumper. 'Where are the kids?'

'Jake's at school and the other two are at nursery.
Why?'

'Because I want to steal you.' She sat on the bed
next to Kate and gave her a diffident smile. 'Ben and
I are getting married on Friday week—I wanted you
to help me buy a dress.'

Kate's jaw dropped, and with a shriek she launched
herself at Liv and hugged her. 'Oh, Liv, that's brilliant! Of course I'll help you—but don't you want to
go to London?'

Liv shook her head. 'No. I don't want anything too
extravagant—just a simple dress. There must be
somewhere local.'

There was. In fact Kate assured her there were lots of places. They left Missy and Kit with Ben for the morning at his insistence, and went dress-hunting, and on the way Kate pecked away at her for details of the sudden proposal and change of heart.

'You told me there was nothing like that between you,' she said crossly. 'Were you lying, you dark horse?'

Liv shook her head. 'No. Just a bit slow to catch on.'

Kate sighed. 'I could die of jealousy. Well, that's not true, I love Andy to bits, but he's not a hunk like Ben. Fancy snuggling up to all that man every night for the rest of your life.'

She did. She desperately did, but it wasn't going to happen, and Kate wasn't going to know! 'Your fantasies are showing,' she said lightly, and Kate laughed.

'I confess. Right, let's find you a dress.'

They went into a big department store in Ipswich and looked through the bridal wear, and drew a blank.

Everything was either too fussy or too plain, or the wrong colour. She needed white—cream looked all wrong with her slightly sallow skin and dark hair— and most of the white dresses looked like meringues.

'Except I'm so vast I look like a pavlova,' she said morosely, and Kate swatted her and towed her off to another shop.

And there they found it, a simple white dress in the softest silk dupion, with a deep V bodice smothered in fine ivory embroidery, long slim sleeves and a skirt that was neither too straight nor too full. The hem was scalloped, as were the ends of the sleeves, and instead of a train the back of the skirt fanned out into a duster train.

It wasn't the dress she would have married Oscar in. That dress would have been straight and slim and elegant, vastly more expensive and suitable for the stick-thin and fashion-conscious woman she'd been four years ago.

Now she was a mother, and the dress was gentler, more feminine, and she felt beautiful in it.

'You look gorgeous,' Kate said wistfully. 'I wish I was getting married again. There are so many lovely dresses about.'

Liv chuckled. 'What about my hair? Do I need a headdress, or should I just put it up?'

'Something simple,' Kate said, scanning the display. 'How about this?'

It was a plaited circle of white silk bands, slightly padded, with fine embroidery on it and the veil coming out of the centre, and it finished the dress off to perfection.

And, Liv thought, I can have the veil over my face when I make my vows, and maybe the expression in my eyes won't be such a dead giveaway.

Ben's mobile phone rang in her handbag, and she answered it, wondering if she'd conjured him up just by thinking about him.

'How are you getting on?' he asked.

She could hear Kit screaming in the background, and smiled at Kate. 'Fine. I think we're finished.'

'Good. I don't suppose you'd like to come home, would you? Kit's getting a bit desperate.'

And, judging by the sound of it, so was he. 'We're coming now,' she promised, and they were back at the house in half an hour.

Kate went to fetch her children from nursery, Ben shot into his study with a hunted expression on his face and Liv settled down with the children and sorted them out, then made a cup of coffee while she fed Kit—she was getting good at multi-tasking, walking round feeding him at the same time as she did things with the other hand.

Missy wanted a biscuit, and although it was too near lunchtime she gave her one, then changed both their nappies. It was really time Missy started potty training, she thought, but with all the upsets over Oscar and with the wedding and Christmas coming up, it didn't seem like a good time to start.

She put Kit into his crib, and held out her hand to her daughter. 'Come on, let's have some lunch.'

She shook her head. 'Missy sleep,' she said, and lay down on the floor with her thumb in.

Liv hesitated a fraction of a second, then scooped the child up and popped her into bed. 'All right, darling. You sleep. See you later.'

She kissed her gently, smoothed her tumbled curls out of her eyes and left the room. Perhaps now would be a good time to tackle Ben about all the outstanding arrangements for the wedding.

She ran down the stairs and tapped on the study door, and he rapped, 'Come in!'

She opened the door cautiously. He didn't sound in a wonderful mood, she thought, but she must have been mistaken because he pushed away from his desk and spun round towards her with a smile.

'Hi. All quiet on the western front?'

She smiled back, relieved that he wasn't still cross about his wasted morning. 'They're both in bed. I wondered what you wanted for lunch, and thought we could talk about the wedding arrangements, if you've got time.'

'Sure.' He stood up and stretched, and his shirt pulled out of his jeans and gave her a delicious and tantalising peep of smooth muscled abdomen arrowed with a fine line of dark hair plunging down below his waistband.

She gulped and dragged her eyes away, spun on her heel and headed for the kitchen. Why did he have to be so infernally *sexy*? she asked herself crossly. He never used to be. Why start now, when she'd committed herself to him for the next however many years of torture, watching him wandering about the place looking stunning and being totally out of reach?

Further out of reach than ever, really, because they would be stuck with each other and it was more than her ego could manage to proposition him and be turned down, even as gently as she knew he would do it.

Damn, damn, damn—

'Has that kettle offended you?' he asked mildly, and she sighed and put it down on the base and flicked it on.

'No. Sorry. Just thinking,' she fobbed, and reached for some mugs. 'Coffee?'

'Thanks.' He stretched out easily at the table and played with the sugar, dribbling it from the spoon back into the bowl. 'So, about the wedding. How many people are we talking about, and what are we going to do with them all?'

She looked at him in puzzlement. 'Do with them?'

'Yes—for the night. I've got six bedrooms in this house. I'm in one, and the kids are in another. They'll all work out that that leaves four rooms—which means your parents, my parents, and my two sisters and spouses and children variously will expect to be accommodated. And make no mistake, Liv, they'll all expect to be here, and they'll all expect us to be together.'

It was something she hadn't even thought of. Hot colour flooded her cheeks, and she whirled back to the kettle and started spooning coffee wildly into the jug. 'So—we'll go to a hotel. We'll say we're having a one-night honeymoon, and we'll go to a hotel and spend the night there in two rooms, and they won't be any the wiser.'

'What about the children?'

She thought hard for a moment, and came up with a wonderful idea. 'A family suite?' she suggested. 'A little room for the children and another room for us? Then we can move around until we've all got some privacy.'

He shrugged and pulled a face. 'Could work, I suppose. How about Missy? Will she settle in a strange place?'

Liv laughed softly. 'I don't know. I hope so.'

'So do I,' Ben said fervently, 'because if there's one thing I am sure about, it's that I don't need my sisters watching us go through my bedroom door on our wedding night and checking us for signs of sleeplessness in the morning! They were always much too curious about my private life for my liking.'

'I don't suppose they'd all like to stay in a hotel, would they?' Liv said wistfully.

He shook his head. 'Not a chance—and anyway, this is better, because they'll expect us to go away for at least one night, and looking on the bright side, it means we won't have to cook or wash up for them all.'

Liv managed a smile. Just a small one before she turned away, because all she could think about was that he was talking about their wedding night, and it should have meant so much more to them both.

'How about lunch?' he said from right behind her. 'Want me to scramble some eggs?'

She poured the coffee and turned to him with a little laugh, handing him his mug. 'Can't you cook anything else? It's all you ever suggest.'

He chuckled. 'Stick with what you're good at, that's my motto. And in answer to your question, no, I can't cook anything else. Why? What did you have in mind? Cheese on toast? That seems to be your standby.'

She bit her lip so she didn't laugh.

'I tell you what, a compromise,' she suggested. 'How about a cheese omelette?'

'Done,' he said instantly. 'And while you do that, I'll make some more coffee that isn't strong enough to strip paint. It's a good job I'm marrying you, or I'd be forced to sack you for dereliction of your culinary duty.'

Did her face fall? Probably, because with a muttered oath he pulled her into his arms and hugged her. 'I was joking, Liv,' he said softly against her hair. 'Don't take the hump. I'm not Oscar. I'm not criticising you. I was just teasing you, sweetheart.'

She relaxed against him, slid her arms round his waist and hung on. It felt so good to hold him, and it was the sort of uncomplicated hug he'd given her a million times before.

How odd, then, that after a moment they should both feel awkward and move away, almost as if, on the brink of their marriage, such feelings were forbidden...

CHAPTER SIX

KATE was in her element planning the wedding. In the absence of anyone she treasured more, Liv asked her to be her matron of honour.

'I meant to ask you yesterday, but we ran out of time,' Liv said. 'I don't have a sister, and we had some great fun at college before I dropped out. You were my best friend, really—well, apart from Ben, but I can't ask him to be a bridesmaid, he'll be a bit busy!' she said with a grin, and Kate chuckled.

'Just so long as I can wear something simple and not a meringue, because I'll definitely look like a pavlova!' she said with a laugh.

'We could always hire a dress—perhaps we should ring up and see if they do a dress to go with mine?' Liv suggested. 'We didn't even have time to look yesterday.' So they rang the shop, and, yes, they did the bridesmaid's version in a variety of colours for hire.

'I'll go in and try them and sort it out,' Kate promised. 'How exciting—I'm going to be matron of honour to a famous model!'

'Huh! Ex-famous model,' Liv reminded her, handing her another cup of coffee. 'Or do I mean infamous? And anyway, there won't be any publicity.'

'You think?' Kate said with raised eyebrows. 'Ben's quite a mover and shaker in the business world. I think you might find if the press gets wind of it, you'll get publicity, especially if they put two and two together and come up with both of you, if you see what I mean.'

Liv did. Still, there was only little over a week to go, and surely none of their few guests would spill the beans?

'Have you told Oscar?' Kate asked, raiding a grape from the fruit bowl on the kitchen table.

'No. On a need-to-know basis, I thought he didn't,' she said drily, and Kate chuckled.

'You really hate him, don't you?'

'He didn't do me any favours, Kate,' Liv said quietly. 'He stole everything I had, everything I was— my money, my confidence, my enjoyment of life—he took it all. His only saving grace is that he gave me my children. It's the only thing that stopped me leaving him ages ago.'

'And now you've got Ben—I always thought he was gorgeous, but in all the time we've lived next to him, I never for a moment thought he could be *your* Ben that you talked about at college.'

Her Ben? The Ben she'd idolised as a girl? He'd moved on since then, had his heart broken, become a recluse, almost. He was the same in many ways, but the sparkle seemed to have gone out of him and she didn't seem to have what it would take to put it back.

'I still can't believe it's going to happen,' Liv said thoughtfully.

'Well, it is. You've bought the dress, ordered the caterers—you have ordered the caterers, haven't you?'

Liv nodded and smiled. 'Yes, Kate, we have ordered the caterers.'

'And you're definitely going to marry the most gorgeous man it's ever been my privilege to meet.' Kate sighed luxuriously. 'You are such a lucky girl,' she said, but Liv wondered if she was, or if the whole situation was just getting out of control and was going to blow up in her face.

Since their hug the other day, Ben had been a little distant. Nothing nasty, not cold or cross or anything, but just a little more remote than usual. She wondered if he was getting cold feet, and resolved to ask him. There was no point in entering into a marriage with so many strikes against it if they weren't both utterly committed to it.

She asked him that night, after they'd eaten and the children were asleep and settled.

There didn't seem a subtle way to bring it up, so being Liv she came right out with it. 'Ben, are you sure you want to marry me?' she asked bluntly, watching his face for any flicker of reaction.

There was none. 'Yes, I'm sure,' he said, his voice firm. 'Absolutely positive. Why? Don't you want to?'

Did she? 'You just seem—I don't know—distant.'

He gave a slightly strained smile. 'Sorry. Lot on my plate at work. It's nothing to do with you, Liv.'

'Promise me you'll say if you change your mind,' she insisted. 'Even right up to the last minute—I don't want this if we aren't both happy with it.'

He stood up and went over to where she was standing with her back to the sink, hands locked on the edge of the worktop, her knuckles white, and drew her into his arms.

'Liv, stop it. It's going to be all right. Trust me.'

And this time there was no awkwardness, no distance, nothing but Ben giving her a hug. She sighed deeply, rested her cheek on his shoulder and let the tension drain out of her.

She'd been so afraid he would change his mind, and he seemed if anything more certain than before.

There was nothing to worry about. She was going to marry him, and all she had to do was find a way of coping with it.

'I've booked a hotel for our wedding night,' he murmured against her hair. 'It's just down the road, and they've got a family suite we can have. It sounds fine. And I've booked a babysitter so we can have a nice leisurely dinner without worrying about the children.'

'Oh.' She moved out of his arms and looked up at him. 'I thought we'd get room service or something. Will we feel like eating?'

'I will, and I haven't yet seen you refuse food in the last few weeks, so, yes, Liv, I'm sure we'll feel like eating,' he teased. 'And stop finding things to worry about. It'll be perfect. You'll see.'

The Friday of their wedding dawned bright and clear and gorgeous. It was mild for the time of year, crisp at first but the sun soon warmed the air and it turned into a beautiful day.

The caterers were there from ten o'clock, and Liv's parents arrived shortly afterwards, having spent the night in London with friends. Her father crushed her in a huge hug, held her at arm's length and hugged her again, tears in his eyes.

'I'm so happy for you,' he said.

'He's been writing his speech for days,' her mother told her, hugging her when he'd eventually released her. 'He's like a cat on hot bricks. The house is lovely, by the way. The flowers look beautiful—did you do them?'

Liv shook her head. 'With these two monsters to look after? You must be kidding. I've been rushed off my feet doing nothing! Missy's into everything now, aren't you, darling?'

'Missy pest,' Missy said cheerfully, holding her arms up to her grandmother. 'G'amma cuddle.'

Grandma lifted her into her arms and gave her a smacking kiss, and Grandad ruffled her hair and beeped her nose, sending her into peals of laughter. Liv handed him his grandson to hold, and made them all coffee in the kitchen.

That was how Ben found them a few minutes later, with Missy and Grandma reading a book, Grandad sitting with Kit on his knee looking proud and happy, and Liv sipping coffee and sticking curlers in her hair all at once.

'Ben!' Liv's mother cried, and reached out her arms to him. He bent and kissed her cheek, shook her husband's hand and tweaked Missy's nose.

'Being a good girl, are you, peskit?'

Missy giggled, and he grinned and winked at Liv. 'Love the sexy curlers,' he said, and her mouth went dry.

He was so normal, so natural, so positively irresistible.

'I thought you weren't supposed to see each other today?' her mother said, sounding mildly scandalised.

'Bit difficult when we're all living here together, isn't it?' Liv said. 'I can hardly drive Ben out of his home for an old tradition. I'll make sure he doesn't see me in the dress until we're in the church,' she promised.

'Janie and her clan are here,' Ben said, looking out of the window. 'And Clare and Martin—that's good.

I'm glad my best man's arrived. Oh, and my parents. They must have been lurking locally, all of them. They've probably been in the pub already.'

Liv looked at herself in the mirror by the back door and sighed. 'They'll have to take me as they find me,' she said flatly. 'I'm on the drag, and I have to do my hair. Kate's supposed to be helping me with it.'

'Oh, she rang. One of the kids was sick earlier, but she thinks it's just because he ate something disgusting in the garden. She'll be round as soon as she's organised,' Mrs Greer said, bustling in with an armful of children's toys and putting them back in the box in the corner.

Liv sighed. Her hair was half in heated rollers, half not, Ben's family were all here and her maid of honour was busy mopping up sick! Terrific!

She needn't have worried. Ben's family knew her so well they just hugged her, kissed her cheeks and told her she looked wonderful.

'You're such sweet liars,' she chided them, and put the kettle on again.

'I don't suppose we could have the kitchen, could we?' one of the caterers asked in the midst of the hubbub. 'Only we've got quite a lot to do, and the dining room's all prepared.'

'Come on, you lot,' Ben said, and cheerfully ushered them all out into the drawing room. Liv put in the last of her curlers, scooped the pins and the heating unit out of the way and put them upstairs, and ran back down, still in her jeans and jumper.

'I suppose you do have a wedding dress?' Janie asked, arching a brow.

'Of course—and Ben can't see it, so unless someone wants to blindfold him, it will have to wait.'

'We'll get you ready,' Clare said, and she was swept out of the room and up the stairs by his sisters.

'Look after the children,' the men were instructed over Clare's shoulder.

'I need to feed Kit before I can get dressed,' Liv protested.

'So feed him. We'll do your hair and your make-up while he feeds, and then we can sort out his nappy and so on while you get dressed. Is he going to the church?'

She shrugged. 'I wanted him to, but he's so small.'

'Do you want him there?' Janie asked, and she nodded.

'I do, really. I know it's silly, but I want them both there.'

'Then they'll be there. There will be hundreds of kids anyway, two more won't make any difference, and someone can always take them out if they scream too loud! Right, what about this hair?'

It was done. Her hair was piled artfully on her head, her veil was fixed, her dress was on and fastened and looked lovely, the shoes were ready and waiting—and Clare was having a crisis.

'You've got a new dress, the hair clips are borrowed from Kate, the garter's blue, but you haven't got anything old!'

'Ben?' Janie suggested, and they laughed, but Clare was still worried.

'I could change my bra,' Liv said. 'Put an old one back on. I'm sure it would be more comfortable.'

'It's your wedding! You have to wear sexy undies; don't be daft. You need something else—hang on.

What about a hair clip? Have you got an old one? Or some old jewellery?'

She nodded thoughtfully. 'I have—a diamond drop pendant that Ben gave me for my eighteenth. It's antique.'

'Perfect. You need something round your neck anyway.'

'Like a noose?' Liv said drily, beginning to panic. The time was ebbing away, and shortly it would all be over.

She settled the necklace against her throat, just as Kate entered the room, and turned to the three women. 'How's that?'

'Lovely,' they chorused, and she sighed with relief. 'I want to talk to Ben,' she said.

'But you can't! You're dressed!'

'I need to—please. He can stand on the other side of the door, but I need to speak to him.'

They trooped downstairs and sent Ben up, and moments later there was a tap on the door.

'Liv? Are you OK?'

'I'm fine. Shut your eyes.'

She opened the door and found him standing there, eyes shut as instructed. He was dressed in a black tailcoat and striped trousers, with a stiff shirt and tie, and he looked gorgeous.

'Are you still sure about this?' she asked him, and his eyes flew open and locked on hers.

'Yes,' he said firmly. 'I'm still sure. What about you?'

She smiled and nodded. 'Yes. Shut your eyes, you're cheating.'

He sighed and closed them, then reached for her

blindly, drawing her into his arms. 'Don't worry, Liv,' he murmured. 'It'll be all right, you'll see.'

Then he let her go, turned on his heel and ran lightly downstairs.

'I thought you were going to call it off for a moment,' Janie said, arriving at the top of the stairs seconds later with the other two in tow.

'Talk about giving us a fright,' Kate chided, hands on hips and looking at her with mock severity. 'Right, I think everyone's ready to go. Andy and Steve and Martin are taking the children between them, and we can follow. Then you and your father will come in the wedding car—and don't forget your flowers!'

'I won't,' Liv promised.

Her mother came up then, stood back and looked at her and shook her head, tears welling in her eyes. 'You've never looked more beautiful, darling,' she said, and hugged her quickly before going back downstairs.

There was a lot of door-opening and shutting, and then they were gone, the house was quiet and her father was waiting for her at the foot of the stairs.

'You look beautiful,' he said fervently. 'I'm so proud of you, and I couldn't have chosen anyone better for you than Ben. I hope you're very happy.'

She conjured up a smile, and was hugely relieved that her father would put any hesitation down to nerves, because the last thing she wanted was to get into any kind of explanation now. 'I'm sure we will be,' she said with much more confidence than she felt, and, taking her father's arm, she went up on tiptoe and kissed his cheek.

'The car's here, we ought to go,' she told him, and scooped up her flowers from by the front door. Then she was in the car, her father beside her gripping her hand nervously, and they were whisking down the drive and off to the church.

As she stood in the porch, she heard the music change, and, taking a deep, steadying breath, she laid a hand on her father's arm, smiled at Kate and set off down the aisle.

Ben was there waiting. He didn't move a muscle until she was beside him, and then he turned his head and winked.

'Hello, trouble,' he said softly, and she felt the tension ease. This was Ben. She knew what she was doing. It was going to be fine.

The service was lovely, and as she made her vows, she felt an inner strength she hadn't known she possessed.

There was only one moment of doubt, when Ben said, 'With my body I thee worship,' and there was a tremor in his voice.

He must be thinking of her, Liv thought, and a great wave of sadness washed over her. Poor Ben, to be so heartbroken that he would give up all hope of future happiness to spend his life with her.

And then they were married, and he was lifting her veil back from her face and lowering his head to kiss her.

'I won't bite,' he murmured, and her mouth curved in a smile just as his lips met hers, and desire shot through her, catching her totally unawares.

It was the briefest kiss, the merest sop to convention, but it drove out all coherent thought and left her mind addled all the way through the photographs.

'I didn't think we were having photographs,' she said blankly, and he winked at her.

'Got to have something to show the grandchildren,' he murmured, and looked up, his smile already in place.

She shrugged. It was no big deal. Photographs she could handle, she thought. She'd been photographed so many times it was ridiculous, and she smiled and laughed and looked this way and that, and stood with one group and then another, and then the wind picked up and they adjourned to the house before everyone lost their hats.

'I can take the rest later,' the photographer announced with satisfaction. 'Shots at the reception are always good.'

And then they arrived, and Ben scooped her up in his arms and carried her over the threshold, and the photographer was there to capture the moment.

'Could you kiss the bride?' he asked, and so Ben stopped there in the porch, halfway over the threshold, and kissed her.

It was the second time, but the first time had been a circumspect peck for the benefit of the congregation and that had been bad enough.

Now, for the benefit of future generations, Ben seemed determined to give it his all. His mouth claimed hers, hot and hard and hungry, and for a blissful moment Liv thought it was real, and that he loved her after all.

Then he lifted his head, winked at her and said to the photographer, 'That do you?' and reality came crashing back down around her ears.

Ben didn't love her. It was all an act, put on to fool their dear deluded relatives, and if she let herself read any more into it than that, she was an even bigger fool than she'd thought.

* * *

It was the longest day of her life. She laughed at the speeches, she made witty remarks and she smiled until her cheeks ached. And then Kit needed feeding, bless his heart, and she slid upstairs, struggled out of her wedding dress and put on her dressing gown and fed him.

There was a tap on the door, and Ben came in, dressed in casual trousers and a cashmere sweater over a shirt and tie, a cup of tea in hand. 'I thought you might want this,' he said softly, and came and sat beside her on the bed, his hand warm on her ankle.

She thanked him, touched that he had remembered on such a frantic day, and he smiled ruefully.

'Don't thank me. It was a good excuse to get away from them all. It's hell, isn't it?'

She nodded. 'It's all the pretending,' she said, and wondered if she sounded as wistful as she felt. 'Still, it's nearly over. We can take the kids and escape soon, and hopefully they'll all be gone by the time we get back tomorrow.'

He snorted. 'I shouldn't bank on it. None of them have stopped talking for a minute. The other guests might leave, but I think our families have settled in for life! I think we'll be hard pushed to get rid of them by tomorrow evening. Still, then at least the place will be our own again.'

'Just think, four weeks ago you were a perfectly contented bachelor,' she said wryly, and he laughed without rancour.

'I was, wasn't I? How odd. It seems light years away. I can hardly remember what it was like.'

'That's traumatic amnesia,' she retorted, and he laughed again, sounding more like his old self.

'Very likely. Still, I have no regrets, Liv. I know

today is a bit of a nightmare, but it'll soon be over, and there were very good reasons for doing this. Don't lose sight of that.'

He reached out and touched the pendant, his finger warm against her throat. 'You wore my necklace,' he said gruffly, and he seemed genuinely touched. His eyes locked with hers, and he smiled sadly. 'You looked beautiful, Liv. Just like a bride ought to look.'

For a moment she held her breath. Would he touch her? Caress her? Make this marriage of theirs a real one? His hand was so close to her naked breast. Would he lower it, brush his fingers lightly over the soft swell, cup the heavy fullness in his palm?

No. His hand withdrew, and he stood up, his eyes flickering to the baby. 'I think Kit's finished. Don't forget your tea,' he said in a slightly strained voice, and went out, leaving her puzzled.

He'd been better about her breastfeeding, and now, he hadn't seemed worried until he'd looked down at Kit. So was it Kit that upset him? The fact that the little boy wasn't his own son? Had he wanted a child with the woman he loved, and been denied? Or, worse still, had she died in childbirth?

No. She would have known. Ben couldn't have kept the imminent arrival of his child or the death of his great love a secret from her any more than he could fly—unless it was when she was first living with Oscar and he was out of touch. Maybe his silence had been nothing to do with Oscar and all to do with this woman, whoever she was? Maybe he'd been in love, and had just naturally dropped out of sight for a while to lick his wounds when it had all gone wrong?

She'd never know—not unless Ben ever told her,

and she didn't think he would. Not for a while, at least.

Kit was asleep, his mouth moving rhythmically every few seconds, then relaxing. She eased him off, rested him on her shoulder and burped him, then changed his nappy and put him in his crib. She'd have to disturb him when they left, but it wasn't time yet.

She changed into the only suitable thing she had for going away, a silk trouser suit with a drawstring waist that fitted where it touched. It was wonderfully comfortable and elegant, and would be perfect for the hotel.

And tomorrow she could go back to her stretch jeans and sloppy sweaters, and get on with her life.

Ben headed for his study and a little peace and quiet. He needed time alone to pull himself together. Today was proving far harder than he could have imagined, and he was feeling frayed at the edges and emotionally raw.

Liv, too, was obviously feeling the strain unbearably, and he just wished it was all over and everyone would go away and leave them in peace to try and get back to normal, whatever that meant.

He opened the door of his study, and Clare looked up guiltily.

'Yes, that's right,' she said into the receiver. 'Yes, bill it to my credit card. Thanks.' She dictated a number, the expiry date and her name, and then thanked the person at the other end and cradled the receiver.

'You made me jump,' she said brightly, getting to her feet. 'I just had to borrow your phone—something I forgot to order. Today was the last day of the offer—you don't mind, do you?' She patted his cheek, and he watched her go out, guilt written in every line of her body.

What the hell had she been up to? he wondered, and then looked at the desk. Nothing obvious there—until he spotted the name of the hotel, the reservation number and the date all neatly written down from when he'd phoned the hotel the other day.

Had she been on the phone to them, plotting something? Nothing would surprise him. He sighed and rammed a hand through his hair. Please God, he thought, don't let them have pulled a stunt on us at the hotel. Not tonight, of all nights.

Not when we're both just this close to going crazy. He'd had enough, but Liv—poor Liv. She'd been thrown out by the man she'd given the last four years of her life to, she'd only just had a baby and was so vulnerable at the moment, and Missy was a demanding little minx, a lot like her mother.

She needed peace and tranquillity, security, protection, peace and quiet—not his sisters plotting some ghastly practical joke.

Cursing himself for leaving the number lying around, he hit the redial button. 'Grange Hotel,' a woman's voice said a moment later.

'Sorry—wrong number,' he said, and hung up with a short sigh. Damn.

He glanced at his watch. It was five o'clock, and time that they could decently slip away. He went back up to Liv and tapped on the door.

'Come in,' she called, and he went in to find her putting a few last-minute things in her suitcase.

'All set?' he said, and she nodded.

'I've packed the children's things, and mine. What about yours?'

'They're done,' he said shortly. 'Shall we go?'

'We ought to go and tell everyone.'

He nodded, less tense now there was an end in sight. He would have been even less tense, of course, if he hadn't caught Clare up to mischief.

He didn't warn Liv. She had enough to deal with, and it might be something and nothing.

They went downstairs and circulated for the last time amongst their guests, and out of the corner of his eye he spotted Janie slipping out of the room. Now what? he thought irritably, and told himself not to overreact.

She was coming downstairs when they emerged into the hall, and smiled brightly. 'You two off?' she said.

'Yes—except there are four of us. Where's Missy?'

Janie shrugged. 'I don't know, to be honest. Andy and Martin had all the little ones in the snug watching telly a while ago.'

'I'll get the luggage,' he said, and wondered if it was his imagination or if Janie looked guilty.

He was getting paranoid! He ran up and fetched their cases, went back for the babies' things and put them all in the car, then went back inside for Liv and the children.

Seconds later they made their escape in a hail of confetti, and he slid behind the wheel, gave a deep sigh and relaxed—until he pulled forward and there was a hideous clattering behind them.

'Damn,' he muttered, and shot Liv a wry grin. 'I think they got to the car,' he said, and they drove to the hotel, tin cans on strings clanking and clattering along on the road behind them in the rush-hour traffic.

Cars tooted and people waved, and he smiled grimly and glared at Liv, who was laughing.

'You wait,' he said, forgetting that he hadn't been going to tell her. 'Clare rang the hotel, and I think Janie interfered with our luggage. We may have a few more surprises in store.'

They did. 'Ah, Mr and Mrs Warriner,' the desk clerk said, smiling broadly. 'Yes, a change of room—here you are—the honeymoon suite. I'll get a porter to help you with the luggage.'

'Damn,' he muttered, and Liv giggled and brushed confetti off his shoulder. More drifted from his hair, and she gave up and leant against the desk, chuckling.

'It's not funny,' he said, but her humour was infectious, and he started to laugh.

'I'm going to kill Clare,' he vowed, picking Kit's crib up and following the porter. Liv fell into step beside him, Missy in her arms, and they went up in the lift and along a corridor to the end. There was a big silver sign dangling on the door, saying, 'Just Married,' and Ben sighed and refused to look at Liv.

He could hear her giggling, and when they went into the room and the porter left them alone, she didn't bother to try to hold down her mirth.

The room was a mass of white frothy lace, and at the foot of the enormous and overdressed bed was a trolley. On it was an ice bucket with a bottle of champagne in it, a flower arrangement and a box of liqueur chocolates.

'How sweet of them,' Liv said through her slightly hysterical laughter, and looked around in amazement. 'Good grief, look at it! Talk about over the top!'

Ben was looking, but not at the decor. He was looking at the furniture, or rather, the lack of it. Instead of the children's room leading off, with additional beds in it, there was an alcove into which had been fitted two cots.

There were two tub chairs, a low table, a little desk and chair, luggage stands and a door leading into the bathroom.

And that was that. No other bed—just the vast, overdone confection of satin and lace.

He raised a brow at it, and looked at Liv. 'So who's sleeping on the floor tonight?' he asked, and her face was comical.

She looked around wildly, looked back at him and said, 'Shouldn't there be some children's beds?'

'In a honeymoon suite?'

She sat down on the edge of the bed with a plop, and stared up at him, all trace of laughter gone.

'We'll have to sleep together,' she said after a moment. 'There's a novelty, on our wedding night.' Her voice cracked a little, and she looked at the champagne. 'Well, we don't have to drive or do anything else that needs us to stay sober, so we might as well drink—open the champagne, Ben. Let's drown our sorrows.'

He twisted the wire cage loose, eased the cork up gently with his thumb and poured two foaming flutes. He handed one to Liv.

'Here's to us,' he said, and raised his glass.

Her eyes locked on his, and he thought he could see a shimmer of pain deep inside them. 'To us,' she said softly, and, lowering her eyes so he could no longer see them, she drank.

CHAPTER SEVEN

SHE was feeling tipsy, but she didn't care. Desperate times called for desperate measures, or something like that. The babysitter arrived at seven, by which time the baby was long asleep, Missy had had some sandwiches from room service and was bathed and lying on her tummy in her cot, bottom in the air, snoring gently.

Liv hadn't changed, and nor had Ben, except to shed his cashmere sweater in favour of a jacket. There was no need, not for a quiet dinner in the hotel and an early night. Ben escorted her downstairs, his hair finger-combed to remove the last of the confetti, and she thought in amazement, He's my husband. It's our wedding night. How very strange.

The dining room was already filling up, but they were shown to a table in the window, and moments later a string quartet settled themselves nearby and started to serenade them with romantic melodies.

She caught Ben's eye, and promptly got the giggles. 'Did you know anything about this?' she asked, and he shook his head.

'I recognise the conniving interference of my older siblings,' he said drily. 'Let them just wait until I catch up with them. I expect this is their wedding present—she said we'd have to wait for it. Let's just hope for their sakes they've left the country by the time we get home.'

'I think it's rather sweet of them,' Liv said with a

little smile, getting used to the looks and the attention they were attracting. She'd hardly been able to set foot in public four years ago without being recognised. Attracting attention was something she'd learned to deal with in her late teens, and she could do it again.

'Relax,' she told Ben, and his lips twitched.

'You are such a good sport,' he said softly. 'What are you going to eat?'

'Don't know. I'm starving. Something quick!'

'Told you.' He grinned and flicked open the menu. 'Stuffed mushrooms with garlic?'

'How sexy,' she said, and her eyes widened. Had she said that? She must have had more of that champagne than she'd realised. 'Um—I mean, I've got to sleep with you huffing on me.'

He gave a tight smile. 'OK. We'll pass on the garlic mushrooms. How about braised celery hearts in cream?'

'Lovely. And do you fancy sharing the lobster for the main course?'

'Wonderful.' He quirked a brow, and a waiter appeared as if by magic, took their order and swept off with the menus.

A wine waiter appeared in his place. 'Would you care to see the wine list?' he asked, flicking it open under Ben's nose.

'No, thank you. I think we've both had enough. Could we have a jug of iced water with lemon, please?'

The waiter smiled, disguising his disappointment, and within moments tall tumblers appeared, together with a tall jug packed with ice and beaded with condensation. 'Let's sober up a little, shall we?' Ben said, and poured them each a glass.

Liv knew it was sensible, especially as she was feeding the baby, but she didn't feel sensible. Perhaps that was because she'd already had a couple of glasses of champagne at the reception, and another two or three just now on a definitely empty stomach.

And her head was going to give her hell in the morning, she realised ruefully, and drained the glass.

Ben said nothing, just topped it up again, and by the time the braised celery arrived she was feeling a little more clear-headed.

'Better?' he asked gently, and she gave a wry grin.

'Yes, thanks. I was on the way out.'

'I noticed. You never could hold your drink and you've been knocking it back somewhat.'

I wonder why, she thought slightly hysterically. It's only my wedding day, and I've married a man I love to distraction and he doesn't even know I exist as a woman.

'Fancy a glass of wine with the lobster in a minute?'

She shook her head. 'No. I don't need it. I might have a liqueur later, or Irish coffee or something.'

The food was wonderful, she had to concede. In fact, apart from the froth in the honeymoon suite, the whole hotel was lovely, and even the honeymoon suite might have appealed if theirs had been a real marriage.

'Penny for them.'

'I was just thinking what a nice hotel this is,' she said, half truthfully, and he smiled wryly.

'Whatever it's like, it has to be better than being at home with that lot. I'd be ready to kill by now.'

She shook her head sadly. 'They just love us, Ben. They love us, and they're really excited because they think it's real.'

'It is real, Liv,' he said in a gruff undertone. 'It may not be a classic love match, but it's a real marriage, don't forget that. I meant what I said today in the church.'

Including 'With my body I thee worship'? she wondered sadly. I don't think so.

She stared into his eyes until her own started to prickle, then she looked hastily away and blinked. 'Thanks,' she whispered. 'So did I.' She picked up her glass, sipping the water with undue concentration while she got her emotions back under control.

They had finished the lobster and picked at something from the dessert trolley, and now the string quartet stood up and bowed and left them.

Ben went after them, thanking them, and she thought she saw him discreetly give something to one of them. He was so thoughtful, and she was sure his thanks would have been sincere and well received.

He came back to their table and sat down again. 'Are you finished?' he asked.

It was only nine o'clock, she thought, and a little flutter of panic filled her chest. All that time locked up in the room with him! She wasn't ready for it, not for the long night lying beside him hardly daring to breathe.

'I ought to go and feed Kit, he's bound to be fretting by now, but after that, I don't mind. Have they got a bar with music?'

He nodded. 'They've got a dance band in the bar,' he said.

'Well, we could listen to them, perhaps, if they're

any good? You stay down here; I'll go and feed him and come back and find you. Where will you be?'

'In the bar?'

'OK.'

She made her way upstairs, and found the babysitter with her feet up on the coffee table, watching television. She put her feet down hastily and sat up.

'The baby's fussing a bit,' she said. 'I was going to ring if he didn't settle.'

'I thought he would be. I've come up to feed him.'

'Want me to do it?' she offered, but Liv shook her head.

'You can't—I'm breastfeeding,' she said, and the girl blushed.

'Oh. OK. Do you want me to go out?'

She shook her head. 'No, of course not,' she said, but perversely, she felt shy in front of the youngster, and took Kit into the bathroom to feed him, perching on the loo seat. It wasn't very comfortable, and by the time she'd finished her back ached.

She changed his nappy and put him down in his cot, and he went straight off to sleep again. All that champagne, she thought, and smiled. Missy was out for the count, too, probably exhausted after playing with her new cousins all day.

'OK, he's done,' she told the babysitter. 'Is it all right if we stay downstairs another couple of hours?'

'Sure,' the girl said. 'I'm here till midnight.'

'Thank you. Ring if there's a problem; we'll be in the bar.'

'OK,' she said, her attention sliding back to the television, and Liv left her to it. She found Ben propped up against the bar, deep in conversation with a group of men, and as she approached he threw back his head and laughed.

It was a wonderful sound, a rich, deep sound that had been all too absent in the last few days. It was good to hear it again.

He looked round then and saw her, and held out his arm. 'Liv—come and meet some friends of mine. Jerry Carpenter, Simon Fortune. Jerry, Simon, this is my wife, Liv.'

They straightened up and extended their hands. 'Liv, good to meet you; you're just what Woodbridge needs,' Jerry said, and Simon raised an eyebrow.

'Rather too good for old Ben, aren't you, my dear? No wonder he's kept you such a deep, dark secret, but I would have thought you'd have better taste.'

'Don't listen to them, they're just jealous,' Ben said mildly, and draped a proprietorial arm around her shoulders. 'Excuse us, gentlemen. We have a wedding night to celebrate.'

He ordered them Irish coffees from the bar, and then they found a little table against the side wall and sat looking at the dance floor. They seemed to have run out of harmless conversation, and the band seemed to be playing a succession of foot-tapping numbers. They launched into a session of rock'n'roll, and finally Ben shot her an unreadable look. 'Dance?' he suggested, and she nodded, desperate to move.

He led her to the dance floor, and she remembered that he'd always danced well. They'd often danced together at parties in the past, and this was no different.

Not really.

Well, not until the music changed, and the band played a slow, sleazy number. Ben hesitated for a moment, then held out his arms and she went into them, hardly able to breathe with anticipation. One hand rested in the small of her back, the other cradled her right hand in a gentle clasp as he folded her into his embrace.

Her head found the hollow of his shoulder, nestling naturally at the base of his throat, and she felt the slight rasp of his beard against her forehead. There was something shockingly primitive about it, something elemental and basic that called to the woman in her.

She felt desire shiver through her skin, sliding over her body and heating it. Her heart beat in time with his, her legs brushed his as they swayed to the music, and they could have been alone.

The song came to an end and slipped easily into another, equally slow and romantic, and Liv closed her eyes and stopped thinking and worrying and trying to pretend, and just concentrated on enjoying his nearness, the solid feel of his body under her hands, the brush of his thighs like steel against her legs.

Someone bumped into her, pushing her against him, and to her astonishment she realised he was aroused. Surely not?

He stepped back abruptly, dropping her like a hot brick. 'Shall we sit down? It's getting a bit crowded, and I could do with another drink.' He sounded a tad frantic, she thought. How curious.

'Sure.' Bemused by his reaction, she followed him off the dance floor, and they discovered someone had taken their table.

'Should we just call it a night?' she suggested, and she wondered if she'd imagined it or if there'd been a flicker of tension in his eyes. 'We could get room service to bring us up drinks, or make tea or coffee in the room,' she added. 'Actually I think there's a bar fridge in there.'

'There is. What a good idea. We can have a night-cap.'

They went up in silence, standing apart in the empty lift, and all the easy camaraderie of the last ten years seemed to have evaporated in an instant.

He paid the babysitter, then turned to Liv. 'Do you want to have a drink, or turn in?'

'I'm quite tired,' she confessed, wondering about the knot of tension that was forming in the pit of her stomach.

'You go ahead and take the bathroom first, then. I'll have a drink and watch the television.'

He went to the mini-bar, pulled out a miniature bottle of Scotch and poured it into a glass, then sat down with his back to the bathroom door and focused on the screen.

With a little shrug Liv opened her case and searched for her nightdress. It was in here somewhere, she was sure. She remembered putting it in—

'Oh, no!'

'What?'

'My nightdress—it's missing. And there's this—I don't know—this scrap of nonsense, about the total day's output of a sickly silk worm!'

She held up the offending garment, and Ben looked at it for a long moment and then closed his eyes and groaned.

'I knew it. I just knew Janie was up to something.' He marched over to his own case, yanked it open and swore. 'They've nicked my pyjamas, and replaced them with this.'

He held up a thong, small enough to make her blush, and then threw it down. 'And what the hell—?'

He slammed the lid down, and Liv frowned. 'What?'

'You don't want to know,' he muttered, his neck going an interesting shade of brick.

'I might.'

'You don't, trust me.'

'I want to know.'

He sighed and opened the case, handing her a jar. 'Chocolate body paint?' she said faintly, and looked at him in despair.

'I told you you didn't want to know,' he growled, and threw the jar into the case. 'When I get hold of them, I'll—'

'What? Tell them off?' she said gently. 'Ben, if it really was our wedding night, I'd wear that nightie for you, and you'd wear the thong, and we'd use the body paint. You can't say anything to them. They were just having fun, and if we hadn't lied to them it wouldn't be anything but a giggle.'

She pulled a T-shirt out of the case, and clean, utterly sexless cotton knickers, and headed for the bathroom with her wash things. Her composure held until she was through the door, and then the tears started to fall, great huge tears that seemed to be dredged up from the bottom of her soul. She turned on the taps, sat on the side of the bath and cried until her throat ached and her eyes burned and her soul was desolate.

Then she heard the door open, and Ben came in and crouched in front of her, his big, gentle hands cupping her face and holding it up so he could stare into her tear-drenched eyes.

'Oh, Liv, I'm sorry,' he whispered, and drew her up and into his arms, rocking her firmly against his chest and holding her as the storm of weeping rose to a new crescendo, and then died away.

'I'm sorry,' she sniffed, pushing him away and reaching for loo paper to blow her nose. 'I'm a mess.'

'You're lovely. Wash your face and come to bed. You need to sleep.'

He went out, closing the door softly, and she washed and changed and went back out in her hip-length T-shirt and chain-store knickers.

He winked encouragingly, took her place in the bathroom and emerged a few minutes later dressed only in a pair of sensible boxers. 'Thought I'd give the thong a miss tonight,' he said with a wry smile, and she gave a tiny, rather weary laugh and climbed into bed.

'Which side do you want?' she asked.

'Doesn't matter. Why don't you have the side nearest the children? Then you can get to the baby easily if he cries.'

She nodded and lay down, and he put on the night-light, a soft glow in the alcove by the door, and then leant over her, his hand caressing her cheek gently.

'I'm sorry it's been such a hell of a day, but it will get better, I promise,' he said quietly. 'It's just because it's our wedding night, and there are so many expectations, and our relationship just doesn't fit the mould. I know I'm not the man you'd choose to be with tonight, but we can't always have what we want, Liv. Sometimes we have to make the best of it, and settle for what makes sense at the time. But I won't let you down, Liv. I meant what I said. I'll be there for you, come hell or high water, as long as you want me.'

But you are the man I want to be with! she wanted to cry, and then the impact of his words sank home. Sometimes we have to make the best of it.

Was that what she was? The option that made sense at the time? And what about later, when it didn't make sense any more? What then? Would he say goodbye, like Oscar, or would they live together and bicker and fight and squabble over every little thing, because all of a sudden it didn't seem like such a good idea any more and resentment was clouding their judgement?

All his fine words now were all very well, but under the pressure of reality would he feel the same? She was very afraid he wouldn't, and it made her desperately sad.

She reached up and cupped his beloved face, and wished she had the strength to draw it down and kiss those frown lines away from between his eyes, and ease the strain she could see around his mouth.

'Thank you,' she murmured, and, closing the gap, she kissed him just briefly on the mouth.

For just the merest moment he hesitated, and then he rolled away, lying on his side facing away from her with the whole of the centre of the honeymoon bed a yawning void between them.

'Goodnight, Liv,' he said firmly. 'Sleep well.'

Not much chance of that. With a stifled sigh she lay back against the pillows, swallowed the tears that rose again to choke her and resigned herself to a sleepless night.

* * *

There was hardly room on the drive when they pulled up at the house the following morning. Ben squeezed the car in behind his father's, and helped Liv carry the children in before going back for the luggage.

'Don't say anything to them,' she pleaded as he set the last case down and headed for the kitchen.

His mouth firmed, but he nodded acquiescence, opened the kitchen door and caught the first of the barrage of children that ran at him.

'Uncle Ben! Is Aunty Liv here? Where's Missy?'

'I want the baby—where is it?'

'Hug! I want a hug! Pick me up!'

'Shh,' he said, laughing and bending down to hug them all in turn. 'Yes, Aunty Liv's here, and the children. Hi, all.'

Liv followed him in, Missy darting in beside him to see her new cousins, Kit asleep as usual in her arms, and the first thing she noticed was Janie and Clare standing together on the other side of the island looking guilty.

'Are we forgiven yet?' Clare said, and Ben gave them a mock glare and laughed without rancour.

'Just about. The room was a little over the top, and we won't talk about the luggage.'

'That was me,' Janie confessed. 'How were the string quartet?'

'Lovely,' Liv said emphatically. 'They were very talented, and they were a pleasure to listen to. Thank you.'

Clare's shoulders dropped inches. 'Thank heavens for that. I thought we'd be lynched.'

'Left to myself, you might have been right, but Liv is more charitable,' he growled. 'She's been interceding on your behalf all the way there and back.'

'Oh. Thanks,' Janie said, shooting Liv a grateful smile. 'Well, we've done what we can to make amends,' she went on. 'We've taken all of Liv's clothes from her room and moved them into yours, Ben, to save her a job. We shoved all your stuff up at one end—do you know you've got over twenty suits? Why on earth do you need twenty suits?'

Liv and Ben exchanged stunned glances.

'He doesn't,' Clare said bluntly. 'Half of them will be out of fashion. Liv, you need to go through his wardrobe and chuck out all the things that don't fit him or are out of date. There's a second-hand shop in the town—take them in there.'

'I know it—they've got a lot of my stuff,' she said a little weakly. 'Um—thanks.'

'Pleasure. Coffee?'

'In my own kitchen?' Ben said in an undertone for Liv's ears only, then louder, 'That would be lovely, Clare. Thank you.'

'I hope you don't mind, but we thought we'd stay until tomorrow,' Mrs Warriner said airily. 'It's so lovely to see Liv again, and we hardly saw her yesterday. Is that all right, Ben? Liv? It's so nice to catch up with Glen and Margaret, as well, after all these years.'

'So are you all staying?' Ben asked, a thread of panic in his voice, and they nodded like a well-trained chorus.

'We thought so, if that's all right. I know it's your honeymoon and all that, but you modern youngsters don't worry about that sort of thing, and it's so rare we all get together,' his father said. 'Which reminds me, you are coming for Christmas, aren't you? It'll be a bit hectic, but it should be fun.'

Liv looked wildly at Ben, and he shook his head. 'Sorry, Dad. We're spending Christmas quietly at home, just the four of us. Liv's had more than enough excitement for one year, and she's tired.'

'We'll get a takeaway for tonight,' Clare said firmly. 'We can't possibly cook for sixteen without hassle.'

Sixteen? Liv thought in despair. No wonder the kitchen felt a bit crowded!

Actually it was a lovely day, in a rather disorganised way, if you discounted the way Ben kept touching her, putting his arm round her, his hand on her shoulder, dropping kisses on her forehead as he passed—little affectionate touches that his family would be looking for and expecting in newly-weds.

It just made it all that much more stressful, though, and there was nothing much to do to keep busy and take her mind off it, because nobody would let her lift a finger. Lunch was left-overs from the buffet the day before, with wedding cake for pudding, and it was simplicity itself because they used paper plates and just threw them out.

The meal that night was harder, a huge takeaway delivered by the local Chinese restaurant, spread out down the centre of the long, formal dining table with wine and laughter flowing and the kids giggling and running round and getting generally over-excited.

Still Liv wasn't allowed to help, and she resigned herself to indolence and had another glass of wine. At least Kit would sleep through the night, she thought.

And afterwards, when the meal was cleared away and they'd talked into the wee small hours of the night, then Liv and Ben had to say goodnight to their guests and go upstairs to Ben's room and spend another night together in the same bed. Somehow, though, with them all just the other side of the door, it seemed much worse.

'I could go back down to the study and sleep on the couch,' he suggested.

'It's about half your length—what good is that? There's a bed in the nursery—'

'And Janie's put Adam and Peter in there, like bookends, one each way. The other two are in the little dressing room off Clare and Martin's room.' He sighed and rammed an impatient hand through his hair. 'Basically, Liv, there are no beds left in the house, and if you want to sleep tonight, you're going to have to put up with me again.'

He looked so miserable she wanted to cry. Instead, she went over to him, put her arms round him and hugged him. 'I've had worse offers,' she said gently, and he laughed and hugged her back.

'You're a good girl. It's only one night. I'm sorry my family are so darned pushy.'

She lifted her head and looked up at him. 'Don't weaken about Christmas, will you?' she pleaded. 'I don't think I could stand them all again quite yet, not when we're living a lie like this.'

He shook his head. 'No, I couldn't, either. Don't worry, I'll stick to my guns. We'll have a quiet Christmas alone, I promise, and just be ourselves.'

She showered and changed in his bathroom, and emerged in a nightie his sisters definitely wouldn't have approved of. It covered her from neck to ankle, the sleeves coming down over her elbows, and it was the pinnacle of maidenly modesty.

Ben looked at it and laughed softly, then followed

her into the bathroom. He, she noticed when he'd finished, was wearing a masculine equivalent.

'What, no thong?' she teased, and he gave a dry chuckle.

'No thong, little Liv. I'd hate to shock you.'

Little Liv. I'm a woman! she wanted to scream, but she didn't. Instead she settled herself down with her back to him, mumbled goodnight and waited for the deep, even sound of his breathing. Then, and only then, did she relax.

'Liv?'

She shifted sleepily, unwilling to wake. It was too comfy—

'Liv? Kit's crying.'

She lifted her hand, and collided with Ben's chest, just inches away. Awareness dawned slowly, and she slowly took inventory.

She realised she was curled into his side, her head on his shoulder, one leg hitched up over his thighs, her body pressed against his side for all the world like a familiar lover, and when she tried to move away, she found her nightdress was trapped by his weight.

'I'm stuck—you're lying on my nightie,' she whispered, and he rolled away, freeing her.

She slid out of the side of the bed, went into the nursery and lifted the crying baby up. There was nowhere to feed him except downstairs or in bed with Ben, and after waking up so intimately tangled, she wanted space.

She headed for the kitchen, and found Ben there, putting the kettle on. 'You don't have to do that,' she protested, but he just smiled.

'Oh, yes, I do. I could kill for a cuppa. Don't you

worry about me, Liv. Just feed the baby before the rest of them wake up and it turns into the Mad Hatter's Tea Party.'

She stifled a laugh, settled in the chair and unfastened the front of her nightie, and within seconds Kit was quiet.

'Here,' Ben said, setting a mug down beside her. He dropped into the other chair, put his feet up on the table and yawned hugely.

'Tired?' she asked, and he laughed.

'Tired of my relatives. They'd better go tomorrow, or there'll be hell to pay.'

He rested his head back, closed his eyes and sighed. 'How about you?' he asked after a moment. 'Are you all right?'

Was she? She didn't know. Like this she was, curled up in the dimly lit kitchen, with everyone asleep except her and Ben and the baby, but when they'd all gone and everything was back to what passed for normal in their strange household, how would she feel then?

'I'll live,' she said honestly. 'I could do with a quiet day or two to get over this.'

He snorted. 'You and me both, Liv. The trouble is, we won't get it. You've got Missy underfoot, and I've got bad weather coming up, road and rail holdups, a whole plethora of public holidays and everyone shopping like mad. I could do with twice as much capacity, half as much aggro and a month in the Azores without my mobile phone.'

Liv chuckled, and Ben shot her a smile.

'That's better. I thought for a moment you'd lost your sense of humour.'

She shook her head. 'No. No danger of that. I'm

just tired and confused, Ben. I'll be all right. We'll all be all right.'

She burped Kit, changed his nappy and put him back to bed, and by the time she went into the bedroom Ben was lying there on his back, one arm flung over his eyes.

She closed the door, slid in beside him and curled on her side facing away from him. She didn't want to risk a repeat of their earlier performance.

However, her body was disobedient and knew where it wanted to be. When she woke in the morning, she was back in Ben's arms, curled like spoons together, her back to his front, and against her hip she could feel the subtle but unmistakable pressure of his arousal.

Careful not to wake him, she eased away, and he released her immediately, rolling over with a sleepy sound of protest. She sighed softly.

It meant nothing. That sort of early-morning reaction was normal for men, she knew—a reflex, as natural as breathing. It was nothing to do with the fact that she'd been in his arms, and her breast still bore the imprint of his hand.

Just reflex, she told herself, and stifled a sigh of regret.

Still, she comforted herself, their invaders would leave today, and they could get back to normal. From tonight she could sleep alone again.

The thought brought nothing but regret.

CHAPTER EIGHT

THINGS got better after that. Ben helped her move her things back into her room, and she had the bed to herself again.

Funnily enough she didn't sleep well without him, but at least she could be herself.

Kit, perversely, started going through the night just as she had to explain to Mrs Greer that Ben's wardrobes were too full for her things, and anyway the baby kept waking and it wasn't fair on him to disturb him every night when he was so busy.

'Whatever you say, dear,' Mrs Greer said in a voice that told Liv clearly that she didn't believe a word of it.

Tough. Mrs Greer was the least of her problems.

The thing that was troubling her most was money. Her clothes had sold, but the small amount she'd received for them, although not insignificant, wasn't enough to provide new clothes for the children.

Missy's feet had grown, and she would need a new coat before the end of the winter. Her arms were longer and sticking out of the ends of her sleeves, and her legs had outgrown all her tights and trousers.

And Kit, of course, was growing like a weed and having to wear all the choochie pink stuff she'd had for Missy when she was a baby. There was nothing wrong with any of it, but it was a bit effeminate for him.

Kate came to the rescue, of course.

'I've got loads of boys' stuff,' she said. 'Come round and have a look.'

'But you might have another baby,' Liv protested, and Kate laughed like a drain.

'Not a chance. Apart from the fact that there's not much danger of me staying awake long enough to get pregnant, there's no way we're having any more. Andy's going to have the snip. Come round now and we'll sort it out.'

So they bundled the children into the buggies and went to Kate's, and all the baby clothes came out and Kate went quite gooey over them.

'I remember the first time Jake wore this,' she would say, and then tell the story.

The pile of clothes grew, despite Liv's protests, and in the end they nearly came to blows because Liv insisted on paying for them.

'No,' Kate told her firmly. 'Have them—borrow them if necessary, but you aren't paying for them. Don't be ridiculous. Loads of them were presents, anyway. It wouldn't feel right taking money for them.'

Liv conceded in the end. 'All right,' she agreed, 'I'll borrow them—and if you get pregnant again before Andy's op, you'll still have them all and I won't have to feel guilty.'

'Unless you have another one, of course,' Kate said blithely. 'I mean, you're bound to want to have Ben's baby, aren't you? I would, if I were you. Sort of cement your marriage and all that—and you can be sure he wants one. Men always want a child to carry on the family name, and he's the only son, of course, so he's even more likely to want to.'

Liv was stunned. It was something she'd never

even considered. Sure, she knew Ben wanted children, but not with her! With whoever had broken his heart, not with a lifelong friend who had lost her figure and couldn't even cope with the housekeeping!

Unless they used other methods to conceive, of course...

She took the clothes home and washed them to freshen them up, because some of them had been packed away for a long time, and while the washing machine was on she laid Kit on a rug on the kitchen floor and took his nappy off. He could kick for a while and get some fresh air to his bottom, and maybe it was time to potty-train Missy.

'How about it, Little Miss?' she said. 'Shall we take your nappy off and see if you can do me a wee in the potty?'

Missy nodded and pulled the nappy off, tumbling bare-bottomed to the rug with her feet entangled in the dry nappy and a delicious giggle rising in her throat.

'Fell down,' she said, and sat up and pulled the thing off her feet. 'Potty,' she demanded, and Liv ran up and brought it down, sitting her on it with a drink of juice and working on the straw principle—in one end and out the other!

It worked. To her amazement Missy stood up a moment later and proudly showed her the wee. 'Missy potty,' she said, and Liv hugged her and emptied it in the cloakroom, and brought it back ready for the next time.

'Shall we put your nappy on until we've got some pants?' she suggested, but Missy was highly indignant, so she left her in the care of Mrs Greer and shot to the supermarket for some trainer nappies, lightly padded pull-ups for the transitional period until she was reliable.

She bought plenty. There was no point in being over-confident, she thought, and while she was there, she cruised down the luxury products aisle and picked up a delicious looking salmon *en croute* for that night.

She would have to ask Ben for more money, she thought on the way home, and guilt pricked at her again. The trainer nappies were expensive, and so were all the others. Was it really fair to expect Ben to pick up the tab for them? After all, she wasn't in a position to offer anything in return.

Not like a real wife. At least if he was coming home at night and making love to her, she'd feel she was fulfilling her part of the bargain. As it was, he came home to chaos, ate an indifferent meal or a pre-prepared and highly expensive one like the salmon, went to bed alone and left in the morning before she'd really surfaced.

What a wonderful life. No wonder Oscar had thrown her out.

She sighed heavily and unloaded the stuff from the car, and went in to find Mrs Greer at her wits' end and Missy distraught because she'd had an accident on the carpet in the hall.

'Oh, darling,' Liv said, scooping her up and cuddling her. 'It doesn't matter. It's only a little wee.'

'Not wee,' Missy wailed, and Mrs Greer gave a shrug.

Oh, Lord. Now they were trashing Ben's carpets! 'I've got you some clever pants—shall we put them on?' she suggested, and Missy nodded miserably. She was tired, and after an hour of running around in the trainer nappy, Liv put her into a proper one and put her down for a rest.

Kit was flat out after his exciting morning on the rug—now in the washing machine because he'd managed to pee all over it several times—and she put him in his cot next to Missy's.

While they were asleep, Liv cleared up the kitchen, washed the floor just in case, and started on the preparation for the supper. The salmon was organised, but she needed to scrub potatoes and prepare some veg.

Before she knew it the children were awake again, and Ben was home early, while Missy was running around half naked after getting off the potty and the toys were strewn all down the hall.

'Hi,' he said, coming into the kitchen with Missy's naked bottom perched on his suit sleeve. There was a scraping, slopping noise, and he stopped dead and looked down at his feet, a comical expression on his face. 'Potty training?' he asked warily, and she nodded in despair.

'For my sins. I thought I'd give it a whirl. I'm sorry, I was just about to empty it, and it's all up your trouser leg.'

'I noticed,' he said drily. 'Never mind, the suit needs cleaning. My sock feels a tad damp, as well.'

She mopped up the wee and emptied the potty, all the while chastising herself silently for not clearing it up straight away. He had enough to put up with, without falling over a potty on his way into the house! 'I'm afraid we had another accident in the hall,' she confessed wretchedly.

'Wouldn't be the first time,' he said calmly, and set Missy down, leaning over and kissing Liv on the cheek. 'You all right, Liv?'

She nodded. 'Sorry about the mess. It's been one of those days.'

He laughed shortly. 'Tell me about it. My secretary's just handed in her notice and said she's leaving in the new year. Her husband's been offered a job promotion to Leeds, and they're going.' He sighed heavily. 'I don't suppose you've got any secretarial skills?'

She shook her head, relieved that this was one job she knew she couldn't do. 'Sorry.'

'I'll get someone. I might steal my contract manager's secretary—she's very efficient. Bit fierce, but I dare say I'll survive. He won't be happy, of course, but he'll get over it.'

He reached across her and stole a finger of carrot from the pan. 'What's for supper?'

'Salmon *en croute.*'

His eyebrows shot up. 'Getting a bit adventurous, aren't you?'

'It's ready-made,' she said, unable to lie about it, and he chuckled.

'Anyone else would have shredded the packaging and passed it off as their own. You're too honest, Liv.'

She made tea and fed the children while Ben changed and made a couple of phone calls, and then she shot the children upstairs, bathed them at the speed of light and put them to bed so she could concentrate on his meal.

Far from claiming it as her own, it was all she could manage not to destroy it in the oven. As it was the pastry was a little overdone, but at least the fish was cooked. She wasn't into sushi.

'It's good,' he said. 'Well chosen.'

She laughed, and he handed her a glass of wine. 'Here—relax a little. You've obviously had a hell of a day.'

'And you haven't?'

'Goes with the territory,' he said with a chuckle. 'So, how's motherhood? Driving you nuts?'

She thought of Kate's remark about Ben wanting a baby, and shook her head. 'Not really. Actually I love it, but it is a full-time job really if you're going to do it properly.'

'Hallelujah!' he said. 'You've realised!'

She gave him a wry smile. 'Everyone else manages to run a house at the same time.'

'No, they don't. Lots of women struggle.'

Kate doesn't, she thought, but Kate wouldn't. Kate had always been horribly efficient.

She swirled her wine round in the glass, and wondered how to broach the subject of another baby. In the end she did it her usual way, straight in with both feet.

'Do you want to have a baby?' she asked him, and he set his wine glass down and cleared his throat.

'What?' he said. He was watching her warily, his expression unreadable as ever. He must be hell in a boardroom, she thought.

'I said, do you want to have a baby? Kate said something about it today—that all men want to have a child to carry on the line, and that of course you must want one because you're the only son—I just wondered.'

'What are you saying, Liv?' he asked quietly after a moment of fulminating silence.

She shrugged. 'Well—I mean, I know you don't want to do—well, we don't have that sort of relationship, but if you want a baby—well, there are other ways. Technology and all that—if you want.'

'I don't think so,' he said, leaning back and lifting his glass of wine. 'I don't think I want a baby that badly. Besides, don't you think two's enough for you to deal with?'

She shrugged. 'It was just an idea. I thought—if one of them was your own, it might make it easier to deal with all the chaos—give you something back to balance the equation.'

'I have no problem with the equation. I like the chaos. It knocks spots off the emptiness—but another baby? No, Liv. Not like that.'

She took a deep breath. 'We could always do it the other way,' she offered, steeling herself for his rejection.

It was gentle when it came—gentle and irrevocable. 'No, Liv. Not without love. It wouldn't be right.'

She swallowed hard and looked away. 'It was just an idea,' she said a little unsteadily. 'I'll get the pudding.'

'I don't want any more; I've had enough. I've got work to do—I think I might go back to the office.'

And within minutes he was gone, and the silence settled down around her like a shroud.

'It was just an idea,' she repeated, and mechanically cleared the table while the tears trailed down her cheeks and dripped onto her hands.

'You're a fool,' she said crossly, scrubbing the tears away. 'You knew what he'd say. Now you just had to go and ruin it when things were settling down again. You're your own worst enemy.'

And she stomped around loading the dishwasher and sorting out washing until after ten, and then fell into bed exhausted. It was after midnight before she heard Ben come in, and the tight knot of loneliness his absence had caused eased a little.

Whatever their problems, she thought, having him around was better than not having him around, and she vowed to make more effort to be uncontroversial and keep his home life on an even keel.

It was the least she could do, if she couldn't give him a child.

She went to the second-hand shop and asked about her clothes, and was given another cheque. 'They're going really well,' the owner told her.

'Good. I have to get my daughter a new coat—I don't suppose you do children's wear?'

'They do down the road—it's a specialist second-hand children's shop. It's a bit hard to find—off the beaten track. I'll show you the way.'

So she went, and ducked under an archway, and found a little shop crammed with wonderful clothes for Missy. She bought her a coat, a hat, a couple of pairs of dungarees and some pyjamas, and went home light-hearted. She'd saved a fortune over the cost of new things, and hadn't had to ask Ben for help. That was very satisfying.

She showed him her purchases later, and his mouth tightened to a grim line.

'I would have bought her all those things, Liv,' he said, and she thought he sounded irritated. It was the dress all over again.

'They're my children, Ben. Why should you have to?'

'You're my wife.'

'Only in name.'

He stared at her, then gave a short sigh and stabbed his hand through his hair. 'Give me strength,' he muttered. 'I thought we'd sorted this out?'

'So did I. I thought you understood my need for independence.'

'Indep—! Dammit, Liv, we're married! There's no need for you to be independent.'

'Yes, there is,' she insisted stubbornly. 'Being married is neither here nor there. They aren't your children; you shouldn't have to support them.'

'I love them,' he said softly. 'I'd be more than happy to adopt them. I don't care if I'm not their biological father, I want to be there for them. I don't want them running round in second-hand gear because of you and your stubborn pride!'

His voice had risen, and he broke off and turned away, sighing sharply. 'I'm sorry. It's difficult for me when you won't accept help. I thought this was something I could do for you all—give you security, shelter, food, clothes—something to give back for the warmth you've brought into my life. But you won't let me, will you, Liv? You won't let me be a part of it. You're keeping me out, and it hurts.'

She swallowed the sudden tears. Was that how he saw it? 'Ben—I don't mean to keep you out, but I just feel like a charity case.'

'Don't be silly.' His voice was soft again, and he reached for her and pulled her into his arms. 'Oh, Liv, don't be silly. It's not charity. I feel guilty sometimes because I bullied you into this marriage for my own ends. At least let me ease my conscience by doing something for the children.'

'You are doing something,' she mumbled into his shoulder. 'You're giving them a home, and your love.

That's immeasurable.' She straightened up, dragging herself reluctantly out of his arms. 'I still need to be independent, though,' she said mulishly. 'I'm used to it—used to having my own money. I hate asking for it and watching everything I buy to see if you'd approve. I want to be able to be frivolous.'

'So be frivolous!' he said emphatically. 'I don't care, Liv.'

'No, but I do,' she replied. 'I care, and I have to live with myself.' She looked down at her hands. 'As I mentioned before, I thought I might try and go back to modelling—just a little every now and then, to top up the coffers from time to time.'

He was silent for a moment, then he sighed. 'It's up to you, of course, but do you really want to go back to that life?'

She gave a little shrug. 'I don't know. It's what I'm good at, what I'm used to. I earned good money, Ben. Why not?'

He didn't reply. Instead he made a cup of tea, took it into the study and shut the door firmly.

She got the train the next day, and then, because taxis were too expensive, she made her way from Liverpool Street Station to the modelling agency on the tube. It was raining when she emerged, and her hair got damp and frizzled up in a fuzzy cloud around her head.

Subduing it with her hand, she pushed open the door and went in, smiling at the girl on Reception. 'Hi,' she said cheerfully, and the girl looked at her blankly.

'Can I help you?' she asked.

Liv blinked. OK. 'I'm Liv Kensington,' she said,

using her maiden name for obvious reasons. The girl, clearly too young to remember the name, stared at her expectantly. 'I'd like to see David.'

'Oh. I don't know if he sees people without an appointment. Normally you have to speak to his secretary—'

'Is that Wendy?'

She shook her head. 'No. Wendy's gone. It's Clara now. Shall I ask her to come down?'

'No,' Liv said. 'I'll go up.'

'Oh, but I don't think you can.'

'I can,' Liv assured her, and headed for the lift. He'd see her, she was sure of it.

He did, but only after he'd kept her waiting half an hour.

'Sorry, darling, I was interviewing—it's been a hellish morning. How are you? I hear you're married—how lovely! Tell all!'

She followed him into his office, with him rattling instructions for coffee over his shoulder at the bemused Clara, and shut the door.

'Actually, David, I wanted to ask you about coming back.'

'Back?' he exclaimed. 'What do you mean?'

How hard was it? 'You know—working again,' she explained patiently. 'Perhaps a few shoots—not as many as before, obviously, with the children, but something—perhaps some promotions or something?'

He looked aghast. 'But—Liv, darling—nobody would want you. You're passé, *chérie*—over, finished. You've been out of the public eye for too long. You're last year's face—in fact, to be brutally honest, darling, you aren't even *last* year's face. And as for the body—well, let's just say that the kids haven't done you any favours. How old is the baby?'

'Ten weeks,' she said tightly.

He eyed her critically. 'Frankly, my love, you need to lose a bit of weight, and even then—I don't know. You aren't going to do fashion modelling again, although there's always catalogue work. You could try that. They're looking for the more mature model, but even then you'd have to do something a bit drastic with yourself—unless you want to try for porn?'

'Porn!' she exclaimed, stunned.

He smiled apologetically. 'Sorry, Liv, but that's the way it is.'

'Coffee!' Clara said brightly, but Liv had heard enough.

'I won't stay, David,' she said with the last shred of her dignity dragged around her like a cloak. 'Thank you for your time.'

'Hey, Liv, you enjoy those children,' he called after her.

She got past the girl in Reception before the first tears fell, but only just. She walked blindly along the pavements, uncaring of the stares of the people she passed. She walked for hours, round and round, until finally she realised it was dark and she was lost.

She hailed a taxi, and asked him where they were.

'Camden,' he said.

Camden? Miles from where she'd started. 'Can you take me to Liverpool Street?' she asked. He did, but it was rush hour and London was gridlocked, and it took most of the meagre cash she had with her.

Then she was on the crowded commuter train coming home, and Ben was there when she got back from the station, his face racked with worry.

'Where the hell have you been?' he asked. 'Mrs Greer had to go home—she called me at the office. Kit's been screaming—I gave him a bottle but he didn't like it, and Missy's been crying—what the hell happened, Liv? Where did you go?'

'To see David,' she said, her voice hollow. 'About modelling.'

'And?'

She swallowed hard. 'He said—he said I'm not even last year's face. He suggested catalogue work.' She couldn't even bring herself to mention his other suggestion.

Ben sighed shortly and pulled her into his arms. 'Oh, Liv, I'm sorry,' he said gently, and it was too much for her. On top of David's words, the long hours of walking blindly round the streets till her feet were almost bleeding, his kindness was just too much.

She cried as if her heart would break, and then pulled herself out of his arms, blew her nose and limped into the kitchen. 'Pig!' she said angrily. 'He didn't have to be quite so bloody honest! Catalogue work indeed!'

She smashed the cordless kettle back on to the base, slopping water over the top, and then sat down and pulled her boots off. Her feet were rubbed raw, a broken blister on one heel had bled onto her tights, and she was exhausted.

'Why don't you go and have a nice long, hot soak, and I'll bring you a cup of tea up when it's made?' Ben suggested quietly.

Because I don't want to look at myself, she thought, but the thought of the hot water was too tempting. 'Where are the children?' she asked.

'In bed. Go on, you've got all evening. Take your time.'

She thanked him, dragged herself upstairs and ran the water, adding copious amounts of bath foam so she could hide under the bubbles. She didn't need any more reminders today of the ravages of childbirth on her body.

'More mature model, indeed!' she fumed indignantly as she slid under the water. 'Anybody would think I was forty-five and a size sixteen! Damn cheek.'

But she knew he was right, and that only the skinny girls were making it to the top—except in 'glamour' photography, of course. There, lush was beautiful, but it wasn't her. She was a mother. She was a wife, even if only in name. She'd been too famous to get away with anonymity, and she couldn't do that to Ben or to the children, never mind herself.

She chewed her lip. There had to be something else—some training she could do. She couldn't go back to college—even she realised she wasn't cut out to be a teacher, and the children were too young.

Evening classes in flower arranging and origami?

There was a tap at the door. 'I've got your tea—what shall I do with it?'

She looked down at the thick layer of bubbles that covered her from the chin down. It wouldn't have mattered if she'd been visible, except for her battered pride. It was quite obvious that he didn't want her or find her attractive.

'Bring it in,' she said, and the door opened and he came in, relaxing visibly when he saw the layer of bubbles.

'Here. Are you feeling better?'

She nodded. 'A bit. I'm still fuming, but I'm coming back down to earth. I'm sorry I worried you.'

'Forget it. I'm going to get you a mobile phone, first thing in the morning. And for God's sake stop killing yourself over this independence issue, Liv. There's time later to worry about that. For now, the kids need you at home, and you need them. Give yourselves time. Give yourselves space.'

He set her tea down on the end of the bath by her head, dropped a kiss on her forehead and went out.

She sighed. He was right. There would be time for independence later. Just now she felt too battered to argue, but she'd keep a tally of what she owed him, and one day, when she'd sorted herself out and got on top of things, she'd pay him back.

Liv Kensington wasn't a passenger, and she wasn't going to start being one now.

CHAPTER NINE

IT WAS a day or two before her feet felt better, and she spent it quietly licking her wounds at home, helping Missy with the potty training and playing with her and Kit.

She was a delight, her little daughter—a sweet, uncomplicated, funny little thing with a delicious sense of humour and a very straightforward way of tackling things.

She had also inherited her mother's stubbornness, and she showed it by refusing to wear the trainer nappies and having the odd accident. Still, without a safety net she was at least instantly aware of any *faux pas*, and within a week she was happily in pants.

She was twenty months old, quite young for such good control, Liv thought, but taking her shopping was now a nightmare. She would fall asleep in the buggy and relax, and whoops! And then, of course, there would be tears and traumas.

Then there was the time she fell asleep on Ben and wet herself and him comprehensively. Bless his heart, he didn't say a word, just carried her out, cleaned them both up and came back down with jeans on in place of his suit trousers, and Missy in a dry set of dungarees.

'Perhaps I should take out shares in the dry cleaners?' he said mildly, and Liv started to feel guilty again. He already had two suits there as a result of the children's accidents—one the potty, the other one

149

of Kit's milky little ~~burps~~—and she had a feeling he must be running out.

'It's a good job you've got so many suits,' she said, and he grinned.

'My sisters don't know the half of it,' he agreed. 'Although they are right—I could do with a few new ones in place of some of the old. If I sort them out, will you deal with it? Give them to Oxfam or something?'

She nodded. 'Sure. Want to do it now?'

'Yes—come up, and I'll try them on and you can tell me what you think.'

Her and her mouth! She spent the next hour watching Ben pulling trousers on and off his long, hairstrewn legs, studied the cut of the trousers over his neat, firm buttocks, watched those broad shoulders shrugging in and out of countless jackets and generally overdosed on him until she was cross-eyed and weak at the knees.

In the end there were two piles—one to keep, one to go out. The 'out' pile was definitely bigger, most of them too small over his broad shoulders and deep chest, but then, as he said wryly, half his decent suits that were in regular use were at the cleaners anyway.

She took the dirty ones to the cleaners the next day, and took the 'out' pile to her second-hand lady. 'Oh, wonderful, they're lovely suits. A bit small, are they? Men usually "grow" as they get older! I'm sure I can sell them for you.'

On her way back up the hill she passed Kate's house, and, taking the car home, she got the children out and went round there. She'd hardly seen her since the London incident, and didn't really know what to say, but she wanted to talk to her to see if she had any ideas about what Liv could do in the future.

'I just feel I'm not using my mind,' she explained over a cup of coffee. 'Does that make sense? I mean, I love the children dearly, and I wouldn't rather be at work or anything, only there must be something I can do—some training for the future, something that uses my brain before I lose it altogether.'

Kate chuckled. 'What, like I have? I always meant to go back to teaching, but I only completed two terms before I had to drop out with Jake, so I doubt if anyone would have me. I'd have to do my probationary year again, at least, as I didn't finish it. Anyway, I don't want to; I find I'm quite content being bovine,' she said with a grin. 'You ought to relax and go with the flow, Liv. It's great.'

'I just want to be independent of Ben,' Liv explained, and Kate sat up and looked at her in astonishment.

'Whatever for? Hell's teeth, Liv, he's loaded! Do you have any idea how big his company is?'

She didn't, but clearly it was enough to impress Kate. 'It doesn't matter,' she insisted. 'It's a matter of principle.'

Kate chuckled. 'You don't want to be so principled, girl. If I was married to Ben I'd be out celebrating my luck in the shops on a daily basis—and I can't imagine he'd mind at all. He seems besotted with you.'

She shook her head. 'No. He's—more of a friend, really. He's just kind to me.'

Kate shot her a look of frank disbelief, and Liv changed the subject quickly. It was getting altogether too close to the truth for comfort.

'Help me find something to do with my mind,' she said firmly. 'And not flower arranging, please!'

'How about Open University? You could do a degree in little bits, made of all the things that interest you. That might be fun.'

Liv wrinkled her nose. Somehow it wasn't what she had in mind. It was learning for learning's sake—she wanted something more vocational—more useful to her in her search for independence.

She picked up the pen on the table and started to doodle on the back of an old envelope. 'I just wish there was something that appealed—something arty, perhaps.'

'You just said you wanted to use your mind!' Kate protested.

'Yes, but I want to be able to work—and don't tell me I don't!' she warned, as Kate opened her mouth again. 'I need this, Kate. I've always been independent. I can't hack being a kept woman.'

'Well, how about going back to modelling again?' she suggested innocently, and Liv nearly told her about David.

She couldn't, though. It was still too raw. 'No. Too cutthroat,' she said, avoiding the real truth in defence of her sanity. 'Something else.'

'I'll think about it,' Kate promised, then promptly added, 'How about selling advertising space?'

'With the kids screaming in the background? I don't think telesales of any sort is possible.'

Kate chuckled. 'No, probably not. Oh, well, forget it for now. What are you doing for Christmas?'

Kate blinked. It was looming ever closer, and she hadn't done anything. She hadn't even sent any Christmas cards yet.

'Nothing,' she said honestly. 'I suppose I ought to go shopping. What do you buy the man who has everything?'

'Sexy undies for you,' Kate said promptly, and Liv coloured.

'I don't think so.'

'Spoilsport.'

She shook her head. 'It's not—we don't—' She broke off, unwilling to talk about the intimate details of her marriage, and finally Kate couldn't stand it any longer.

'You don't what? Wear sexy undies?'

She shook her head, the need to share her unhappiness suddenly more important than keeping up a front. 'We don't sleep together,' she said in a rush. 'It's not that sort of relationship.'

Kate stared at her aghast for a moment, then sighed and reached out a hand. 'But—I thought you loved him?'

'I do,' she said miserably. 'And in his way I'm sure he loves me, too—but not like that.' She let out a shaky breath. 'He doesn't find me attractive. I don't know if he ever will, but at the moment, certainly, this soon after the baby, I don't have a lot to offer.'

'Tosh,' Kate said bluntly. 'You're gorgeous. What are you talking about? If he doesn't fancy you, he must be gay!'

She shook her head. 'He's not gay. There was someone in his past—he won't talk about her, but he said love like that only comes once in a lifetime. That's why he married me. After Oscar I was so battered there was no way I was going into another relationship for years and years, and he knew that. It was a way of giving me security for the children and

getting company for him—killing two birds with one
stone, so to speak. It's not so bad, Kate. It sort of
works—but sometimes…'

She ran out of words, and Kate sat back and stared
at her in astonishment. 'You really married that gorgeous man in some kind of cold-blooded *arrangement*?' she said in a shocked voice.

She shrugged helplessly. 'It seemed like a good
idea at the time, but then I realised I was in love with
him just before the wedding, and I thought, maybe
one day—but then I asked him about having another
baby, and he said, "Not without love," so he obviously doesn't love me or he would have said yes.'

Kate stood up and came round the table and hugged
her. 'Oh, Liv, I'm sorry,' she said gently.

Liv straightened. 'So—not sexy undies, then. Any
other ideas?'

Kate shook her head. 'Gloves? Scarf? I don't
know—socks? That's a good old standby, and nobody
could accuse you of trying to seduce him with socks.'

Liv smiled, as she was meant to, and then she took
the children home, gave them lunch and put them to
bed because they were getting fractious. Then, because it was hours before Ben was due home, and
because David's words still hurt her and the mirror
didn't lie, she went into Ben's little gym and looked
blankly at the equipment.

Where to start? Most of it was weight training stuff,
but there was a treadmill and she'd sometimes heard
him running on it. She stood on the belt, studied the
buttons and pressed 'Start' cautiously. It began to
move backwards, and she had to take a step to avoid
falling off the back.

There were up and down arrows, and she pressed

the up and found the belt accelerated. She warmed up at a walk for a minute, then pushed the speed up until she was jogging.

Not for long. She pressed the down arrow, slowed the thing to a halt and climbed off, her legs trembling. She'd been on it for about two minutes, and she was shattered. Her chest was heaving, her legs were like jelly and her head was pounding.

Not fit enough, she thought, and decided to start with walking, pushing the speed up until she was doing four miles an hour. That in itself proved quite an achievement, she discovered when she'd got her breath back and tried again. Still, she could feel the muscles working, and dimly remembered that she ought to do stretches before taking exercise.

She remembered it again later, when she bent to pick up Kit and felt the pull in her hamstrings.

Still, given time she'd get better. She'd do stretches first, and perhaps have a go at some of the other stuff—some tummy work, for instance. There was one of those frames that you rested your head on and pulled up, instead of doing trunk curls. They were supposed to be better for your neck. She'd try it— perhaps tomorrow.

She heard the door open and shut, and looked quickly round for the potty, but it was safe. Empty, dry, and over by the toys. Missy got to her feet and ran to greet him, and he came into the kitchen with her hands splattered against his cheeks, squashing his face.

He blew a raspberry at her, and she giggled and kissed him to silence him.

'That was nice and juicy,' he said wryly, setting her down. 'How's Mum today?'

He leant over and kissed her cheek, and she suppressed a sigh and smiled at him. 'Fine. How are you?'

'Harassed. My contract manager is threatening to mutiny if I take his secretary, so I'm interviewing. There are several prospective candidates, all too young and inexperienced, all bright-eyed and bushy-tailed and full of empty promises, and at the first sign of overtime they'll all high-tail it to the nearest union rep and bleat about how hard I am!'

'Are you?'

He laughed without humour. 'I'm a pushover, Liv. I'm so easy-going it's ridiculous. If they want time off, if it's reasonable, I give it to them on full pay— and I pay them well, too. I expect a certain standard, sure, but it's a high-powered job and I don't think that's unfair. I keep my temper, I don't rant and rave and shout at them, I don't criticise unnecessarily— some of my managers are tyrants. Julie wants to work for me, I know that, but John just won't let me take her.'

'So just tell him,' Liv said, astonished. 'You're the boss.'

He shook his head. 'It doesn't work like that, Liv. We're a team. We have to work together—and his secretary is an important member of that team. I just feel she's wasted, and one of these young girls would be better as his secretary—less challenging.'

'So tell him that,' she repeated. 'Talk it through. He must be able to see—'

Ben snorted softly. 'He can't see anything except losing Julie. I don't think he can handle the idea of having to break in another secretary, but you're right,

I should just tell him this is how it's going to be. Perhaps if I give him a pay rise he'll shut up.'

'Does he deserve it?'

Ben chuckled. 'Probably not. I don't know. He had one recently.'

'Then just tell him, and get a new girl in early to learn the ropes from Julie before you steal her. Let's face it, Ben, secretaries come and go, and it's not as if Julie's going to be out of the office. She'll still be around if the new girl comes unstuck.'

He nodded. 'I tell you what—how about you telling John?' he said with a wry smile. 'I'm sure he'd understand better.'

Liv arched a brow and put the kettle on. 'Tea?' she offered. 'That's my department. You handle your own staff crises, I've got enough on my plate.'

He gave a mock sigh and pulled off his tie, shrugged off his suit jacket and hung them on the bottom of the stairs. 'You're absolutely right, of course, and I know you are. I'm going to make a phone call. If you hear me yelling, ignore it. I'm going to talk to John.'

He came back a few minutes later, looking dubious. 'Well, I did it. I told him. He was a bit shocked, but he's accepted it. I think he felt if he made a fuss I'd back down, because I usually try and listen and be reasonable. Still, he'll get over it. He knows she's good, and deserves the promotion, and I put it in such a way that he'd feel a heel if he didn't let her go. Still, he'll get a new addition to his office.'

'And you get Julie.'

He smiled. 'And I get Julie,' he said softly. 'Thanks, Liv. You're a star.'

'You knew you were going to have to do it in the end,' she pointed out, and he laughed.

'How well you know me,' he murmured. 'Right, how about letting me put the children to bed while you get supper? I'm starving—in fact, how about getting a takeaway?'

Dereliction of duty, she thought guiltily, remembering that she'd forgotten to take anything out of the freezer again.

'I can make something,' she protested. 'All this fast food isn't good for us, and I have to do something to earn my keep.'

'Not again!' he exclaimed, and shook his head. 'Liv, will you stop beating yourself up over this? Put the kids to bed; I'll get something.'

He went out, and came back a short while later with an Indian meal. It was delicious, but David's words rang in her ears. She wasn't going to lose a couple of stone if she kept eating like this, so she avoided the sauce which was running with oil, had only a small portion of the meat dish, lots of the vegetable accompaniments and a big pile of boiled rice so her plate didn't look so bare.

She got away with it—just. Ben glanced at her, looked at the foil trays and offered her more. 'Oh, I couldn't. The portions were very generous,' she lied glibly, and pushed the rice around on her plate to make it disappear.

He finished the lot, opened a bottle of wine and poured her a glass.

'I shouldn't,' she said. 'Not while I'm still feeding Kit.'

'Just one won't hurt you.'

It didn't seem possible to protest, so she took the

proffered glass, toyed with it until he disappeared into his study and then poured it down the sink, filling the glass with water and drinking that instead.

She checked the children, went back down to the snug and put the television on to watch the news. Nothing caught her attention, and so she went and tapped on the study door.

'Should we be sending Christmas cards?' she asked him, and he looked at her in amazement.

'My secretary's done it.'

'What—even your family ones?' she said, horrified.

He looked vaguely uncomfortable. 'Well—no. I haven't got round to it. I don't suppose you'd like to?'

'Have you got any cards?'

He shook his head. 'No.'

'I'll get some tomorrow. Are you coming to sit down this evening?' she added, and could have kicked herself for sounding wistful.

'No,' he said, clearly distracted. 'I've got to finish this. Sorry. I'll be hours.'

He wasn't looking at her, even, his attention fixed on his computer, and she gave up. Early night, she thought, and fed Kit, took a book and climbed into bed. She was asleep in minutes.

Christmas passed uneventfully. Ben was at home instead of in the office, but otherwise it was much like any other time, except for Christmas Day itself.

For Missy, it was the first Christmas she was aware of, and she loved it. Ben had bought her new shoes and a pretty dress, without tolerating any argument, and a lovely bright red and yellow plastic car. It had a real door, and a roof, and a steering wheel and pedals, and she thought it was wonderful. Ben showed her how to climb inside and pedal and steer it, and soon she was charging up and down the hall.

Her steering was a bit hit and miss, though, and after a couple of days the paintwork in the hall was starting to show the scuff marks. Liv confined her to the kitchen, and cleared all the other toys out of the way to give her room, and she drove round the kitchen table going 'Toot toot!' and giggling her head off.

The exercise made her tired, which was good, because Ben was back at work with Julie, and Liv was in the gym whenever the children were asleep, running on the treadmill and using the trunk-curl frame.

And it was working. She'd cut down on her food, eating only fruit until Ben came home and then having smaller portions of anything fattening. If he asked why she wasn't having pudding, she lied and told him she'd had cake at Kate's or something. And bit by bit the weight was creeping off, and her body was growing more toned.

She was tired, though, and Kit was starting to get restless because her milk was dwindling. He was nearly four months, and she spoke to the health visitor about introducing solids.

'Good idea,' she said. 'Nothing too much, but a little gluten-free cereal would be OK.'

So she started feeding him a sloppy rice-based porridge, and gave him a bottle at midday instead of a breastfeed, because she didn't want him to suffer.

And soon, she thought, he won't need me all the time and I could leave him with someone and go and do a course one day a week.

She looked into the available courses at the local

colleges, but there was nothing. Halfway through January all the spring term evening classes had gone back, and nothing vocational ran for just a term.

Besides, there was nothing that took her fancy.

And then one day Kate came round when she was telling Missy a story at the kitchen table, and she sat and watched as Liv drew a picture to illustrate her words.

'And the little dog curled up on the cushion and went fast asleep.'

She drew in a patch over the dog's ear, filled in its little black nose and put the pen down. 'There.'

'You're amazing,' Kate said, awestruck. 'Do you have any idea how good your drawings are?'

Liv looked at her friend in astonishment. 'Good? No, they aren't. They're just little scribbles.'

'No, they're not—and that was a lovely story. If you're still looking for something to do, why don't you do that?'

'Do what?' Liv asked, wondering what on earth Kate was getting at.

'Write and illustrate children's books,' Kate said patiently as if she were talking to an idiot.

'All right, all right, I'm not retarded!' she protested. 'I just can't believe you mean it.'

'Oh, I mean it all right,' Kate said. 'Have you seen these children's books? They're tiny, slim little things, with bright illustrations and damn all storyline, and they sell for loads of money. They make lovely presents, and we've got hundreds in the house.'

'But could you make a living at it?' Liv asked doubtfully.

'Of course!' Kate exclaimed. 'I've got a friend that does it—I'll ask her. She's brilliant.'

Liv looked at her little doodles thoughtfully. 'Do you really think I could be good enough? I just do this with Missy because I enjoy it. I tell her stories, and draw pictures, and she seems to love it, but it's only a bit of fun.'

'That's the best sort of job, isn't it? One that's fun. Fancy being paid for doing what you enjoy. It knocks spots off stacking shelves in the supermarket!'

Liv chuckled, but her mind was working hard. If Kate was right and there was a market for her talent, then it was something she could do at home. She could have a drawing board set up in the corner of the kitchen, by the window, and she could work while the children played around her feet, and she could try out ideas on them.

'Will you find out for me?' she said, hardly daring to hope.

'Sure. I'll ring now—can I use the phone?'

Within minutes she had the name of a publisher, and Liv rang and asked if they could send her guidelines for how they wanted unsolicited work submitted.

'I have to do a series of illustrations and send them in with the script, but it's the illustrations that they're most concerned about.' She had an idea. 'Could I look at some of yours and see what I'm aiming for?'

'Absolutely,' Kate agreed, and later that morning she brought round a carrier bag full of books and told Liv which were the most successful. They ranged in target age from one to five, and covered a huge range of subjects—and Liv looked at them and thought, I can do this.

She was dying to tell Ben, but she didn't. She wanted to be able to tell him if and when she succeeded. She'd had enough knock-backs to last her a lifetime, and if this was going to be another, it was going to happen in private. Tomorrow she'd go and buy some art materials, and then she'd start.

For now, though, she would go on with her fitness programme. She put the children down for their nap, went into the gym and worked on her trunk curls, then went on the treadmill for half an hour. By the time she finished she was so exhausted she was shaking all over, so she warmed down for a moment then did her stretches.

Enough was enough for one day, she thought, and then as she was emerging, dressed only in leggings and a vest top with sweat running down her body and dripping off her face, Ben appeared in the kitchen doorway.

His eyes raked her from head to toe, and he frowned. 'What on earth are you doing?' he asked.

She would have blushed, but she was already puce from the workout. 'Getting fit,' she said, still a little breathless. 'You got a problem with that?'

His eyes trailed over her again, lingering here and there until she wanted to curl up in the corner and die. When he looked up, his eyes were blazing. 'You're exhausted,' he said angrily. 'No wonder you can't do anything round the house—you're wearing yourself out! And what about the baby? Is this why he's on solids? Because you've run out of milk?'

'He's four months—'

'You're wiped, Liv! You look like hell. What are you thinking about? And you're getting skinny— aren't you eating? You've been having less and less— what are you having during the day?'

'Not a lot,' she admitted, unable to lie and unable to see why she should. 'It's my body, Ben. If I want to starve it and work it, I will, and you can't stop me.'

'Watch me,' he said grimly, and he went through to the little gym, locked the door and took the key out. 'You're banned. The baby's too young for you to tackle fitness training. Walking's quite adequate. Take the buggy out and push it up and down hills— that'll keep you fit. And eat, woman, for God's sake! What was the last thing you had?'

She sighed. 'An apple.'

'And before that?'

'A banana.'

'And before that?'

'Supper.'

He let his breath out on a harsh gust and glared at her. 'You are a fool. Put the kettle on and put some toast in. You are going to eat and drink something sensible, and I am going to stand over you until you've done it.'

'What if I won't?' she said childishly.

'You don't want to find out,' he said grimly. 'I'm going to change—where are the children?'

'Asleep. I only ever do it when they're asleep.'

'Time Missy didn't have a nap, then, isn't it? She can keep an eye on her stupid mother.'

'Don't call me stupid!' she yelled after him, following him up the stairs. 'Don't you dare call me stupid just because I want my figure back instead of this lump of lard and I'm not ready to be thrown on the scrap heap!'

He stopped dead and turned, and she cannoned into him, leaving sweat marks down his shirt.

'You aren't a lump of lard,' he said gently, cupping her shoulders in fingers that sent shivers over her damp skin. 'You're a beautiful woman—and you're a mother. You have to look after yourself. Just eat sensibly and keep moving—you don't have to do this to yourself, Liv. You have different priorities now. You aren't a model any longer. You're a mother. You have a duty to your children. That's much more important.'

A lump rose in her throat, and she swallowed hard. He was right, of course, but—'I just want to look better—'

'You do look better,' he said emphatically. 'You look much better with a bit of weight on you. You looked like a refugee before. Now go and shower, and I'll make you something to eat.'

She went and showered, and changed into her jeans and sweater, and thought all the time that if she really looked good, he wouldn't be able to keep his hands off her. And that was the trouble, of course. It was all very well him telling her she was beautiful, but if he really meant it, would he be able to resist her quite so easily?

No. He wouldn't. He'd be knocking her door down every night and driving her wild with his body.

'Your fantasies are showing,' she said crossly, and stomped down to the kitchen. The table was laid with tea and toast and butter and jam, and Ben was sitting there like a school prefect with an implacable expression on his face, and she gave in.

She wasn't going to make it as a model, he didn't want her—she might as well eat. It wasn't hard. She was starving.

She ate three bits of toast, had two cups of tea and then glared at him. 'Better?' she snapped.

'Much.' He smiled wryly. 'Much better. And to-night I'm taking you out for dinner.'

Her eyes flew up to meet his. Had it worked? Had he finally noticed her? Hope soared—and then his next words brought it crashing down in flames.

'I want you to meet Julie—my secretary. Look on it as a sort of thank-you for getting us together.'

A chill stole over her. Why was it, she thought, that it sounded so ominous? Getting them together sounded—intimate?

Oh, Lord. Surely not.

And yet, she thought, why not? He was a normal, red-blooded man. Just because she did nothing for him and he was fond of her and respected her, that didn't mean he didn't want to have a sexual relation-ship.

Loads of men had affairs with their secretaries.

Take Oscar.

Fear rose in her throat. No. Please, no, she thought. She didn't want to meet her—didn't want to see the woman's quiet smirk.

'I can't,' she lied frantically. 'Not tonight. Missy might be getting a cold—and I've got letters to write. Maybe another time.' And without waiting for his re-ply, she stood up, cleared away their plates and ran upstairs.

Kit started to cry right on cue, and by the time she'd got both children up and put Missy on the loo and found some pants, Ben had gone out again.

She found a note on the kitchen table. 'Gone back to office. Don't cook for me—taking Julie to dinner as planned. Make sure you eat. Ben.'

And then, of course, she found herself regretting

her impulse, because without meeting Julie she couldn't evaluate the opposition.

'What's the point?' she asked herself bitterly. 'It doesn't matter if Julie has three heads—he doesn't even know you exist.'

Instead, she'd settle down and start drafting a few ideas for illustrations. If Ben was going to go down the same road as Oscar, then she needed a career to give her independence, because she couldn't go through all that again lying down.

Not even for the children.

CHAPTER TEN

THE illustrations kept her busy for the next couple of weeks. Every time the children were asleep, now, instead of working out in Ben's gym, she would get her pens and paper out from the top of her wardrobe and work on them at the kitchen table.

Ben seemed to be out late more and more often, and she didn't want to examine too closely why he was coming home after dinner on so many nights. She'd been there, done that, with Oscar.

The dinner with Julie was never mentioned again, but she hovered over Liv like a spectre. Nor did he offer to take her out again, either alone or with anyone else, and he didn't involve her in any of his corporate entertaining, although she knew he was doing it when necessary.

So she tuned out her personal feelings, was civil and polite to him but nothing more, and day by day she added more illustrations to her portfolio.

She tried her story out on Missy in the draft stage, and she giggled and said, "Gain!" High praise from a baby. She tried another, with the same response.

She tried them on Kate's children, and they nagged Kate incessantly to hear Liv's stories again.

Wow, she thought. Maybe I really can do this.

So she finished preparing the story she'd decided to submit, parcelled it all up and sent it off. She'd put Kate's address down with her permission, because she didn't want to have to explain herself to Ben—most particularly not when she was rejected!

And then she waited.

And waited, and waited. January had turned to February, and then to March, and Ben was out late almost every night. When he wasn't out, he was in his study, and any conversation they had was stilted or about the children.

And then a letter came. Kate pounded on her door one morning, when she was clearing away the breakfast things and thinking about going shopping, and when Liv opened the door she thrust the envelope at her and watched expectantly.

'Open it!' she demanded, and with shaking fingers, Liv slit the envelope and pulled out the single, folded sheet.

Dear Mrs Warriner,

Thank you for submitting your illustrations and storyline to us. We have examined them with interest, and wonder if you would like to come down to the office to meet us and discuss your work. Please phone the office to arrange a convenient time, and make sure you bring your portfolio with you to the meeting.

Yours sincerely...

She looked up at Kate. 'Oh, my God,' she said hollowly. 'They want me to go and talk to them about it.'

'Oh, Liv, that's fantastic!' Kate shrieked, and threw her arms round her. 'Oh, Liv! I'm thrilled for you. Let me take the kids to school and playgroup, and I'll come back and you can fix a time to go and see them—I'll have the kids for you, so you don't have to worry. Oh, Liv, I'm so excited for you!'

And she bounced off, waving cheerfully as she gathered up Jake and the buggy and set off down the hill to school.

Alone in the quiet hall, Liv looked down at the letter in her hand and felt a little knot of excitement start to form. Was this it? Would it be the answer to her future?

Because she couldn't stay here with Ben indefinitely, that was for sure. She told herself she had no rights over him, but every time he was home late or she heard Julie's name mentioned, her heart bled a little more.

Kate was back in less than half an hour, and she entertained Missy and Kit while Liv, trying to sound professional, rang and made the appointment for the following Tuesday at eleven. That meant she could leave after Ben had gone to work, and if she got away from the office by one, she'd be back in Woodbridge by three-thirty or four—just in time to get his supper.

And if it was a disaster, he need never know.

She was nervous. Very nervous, so when Ben rang on Monday evening and said he'd been held up and wouldn't be home until late, she was hugely relieved because it meant she didn't have to pretend.

The children were in bed and she was just sorting through her wardrobe for the thirtieth time and debating what to wear the next day when the doorbell rang.

She glanced at her watch. Seven-fifteen. Probably someone collecting for charity, she thought, and went down and opened the door. A pretty, dumpy little woman in her late thirties was standing there, a sheaf of papers in her hand.

'Mrs Warriner?'

'Yes,' she said cautiously.

'I'm Julie Bream—Ben's secretary? I just thought I'd drop these off. I stayed late to finish them for Ben, and I promised he'd have them tonight. We were just passing and I thought I'd drop them in. He said he'd be home early, so he'll have time to look through them. To be honest, I was hoping to meet you—Ben's said so much about you and the children, and he's got these lovely pictures on his desk of you all from the wedding, and—well, I just wanted to say hello.'

'Oh. Um—hi,' Liv said a little blankly. 'He's not home.'

Julie looked startled. 'Really? Oh, I must have misunderstood. Maybe something came up. Well, I'm sure he won't be long.'

'No,' Liv murmured. 'Well, thanks. I'll make sure he gets them.'

'Oh, it is nice to meet you,' Julie went on cheerfully. 'I'm sorry you missed dinner in January. We really enjoyed it, especially Paul. He says he feels much happier about me working for Ben because he's a family man, and—well, John used to flirt and it's not nice, is it? Sort of spoils the relationship. Anyway, I have to go; Paul will be getting impatient. It's our wedding anniversary and he's taking me out for dinner, and it's not often I get to enjoy him in a suit these days, so I'd better make the best of it! Lovely to meet you.'

And she turned, with a little wave, and ran back to the car, slipping in beside her husband.

Liv stared after them. That was Julie? That warm,

sweet, very married woman was *Julie*? She was so up front and open she couldn't lie to save her life, Liv thought. There was no way he was having an affair with her.

She thought of all the emotion she'd wasted on the woman over the past few weeks, and could have kicked herself. If she'd gone to the dinner, she would have found out nearly two months ago, instead of which she'd tortured herself all this time!

Which didn't explain, of course, where he was tonight. Julie thought he was at home, Liv thought he was at work, and all the time he was somewhere else.

But where?

She realised how far they'd drifted apart from the easy, sharing relationship they'd had at first when she'd turned up on his doorstep in the middle of the night. He'd been so caring and affectionate in those days, and now it seemed they could hardly share a civil word.

He came in at ten, and she handed him the papers from Julie on her way to bed. 'Your secretary dropped these round,' she said in an expressionless voice. 'She said you left early to come home. She was surprised you weren't here.'

He scrubbed a hand round the back of his neck. 'I had to go to a meeting in the end,' he said smoothly, but she felt he was lying and her spirits dropped again. 'Right, I'd better look these over. Are you off to bed?'

She nodded.

'I'll see you tomorrow, then. Goodnight.'

That was it. No smile, no goodnight peck on the cheek as he would have done not so very long ago. Just 'goodnight' and that was that.

Oh, hell.

She went to bed, stared at the ceiling until nearly four and then had to rush in the morning. She used copious amounts of concealer to disguise the bags under her eyes, and dressed in her most efficient outfit. She all but threw the children at Kate, kissed Missy who started to cry, and then leapt into the car and drove like a bat out of hell for the station.

She caught the train by the skin of her teeth, struggled with the portfolio in the aisle and then had to fight her way through the underground with it. By the time she arrived at the publishers she was frayed at the edges but just about on time, and as she sat in Reception and waited for someone to come down for her, a mass of butterflies took flight in her stomach.

What if they hated her portfolio? What if they wanted her to change everything, and then didn't like it? What if—?

'Mrs Warriner?'

She looked up, and a young woman in very relaxed clothes came towards her. 'I'm Trudy. Come on up. The others are all waiting—we're very excited.'

Excited? she thought. What about?

She soon found out.

'Mrs Warriner, we love your story,' the senior editor told her. 'It's warm, it's fun, it's colourful—a bit too colourful, in fact. We'd like your permission to reduce the palette for production reasons. But apart from that, it's wonderful. The trouble is, we don't want to give you tons of publicity and do a massive launch if it's going to be a one-off, so—anything else that you could follow it with?'

She dragged in a deep breath and stared at them all, then let it out in a rush. 'Um—yes, sure,' she said.

'I've brought another couple in my portfolio—I wasn't sure what you wanted, so these are a little different, but I thought it might give you an idea.'

They pounced on her work, exclaiming and laughing, and when they looked up their eyes were shining.

'These are incredible,' Trudy said. 'You have such a talent, Olivia—may we call you Olivia?'

'Liv,' she said, and one of them clicked her fingers in recognition.

'Liv Kensington—of course! I thought you looked familiar! Wow! That's so unfair! All that talent in one person! I'm really jealous.'

Liv laughed softly. 'Don't be,' she said. 'I'm just a very ordinary person.'

'I think we can dispense with the modesty,' the senior editor said bluntly. 'You have a very real talent, Liv. We'd like to take you on board—if you'd care to join us. We just have to negotiate the rate. I thought we could do that over lunch?'

'Lunch?' she said blankly.

'Is that a problem?'

She shook her head. 'No—I don't think so. Could I ring my neighbour? She's got my children.'

'Of course—use this phone.' They gravitated back to her portfolio contents, and she rang Kate.

'Can you be a love? They want me to go for lunch.'

'Wow! Go for it. That sounds really promising!'

'It is. I'll talk later. Thanks.' She cradled the phone. 'It's all right. She can keep the children.'

'Excellent.' The editor rubbed his hands together, smiled at her and ushered her towards the door. 'We'll leave this lot planning the scheduling. They're well away. Do you mind leaving all this stuff with us? We can send it back to you—I'll get my secretary to itemise it and give you a receipt.'

'What about copyright?' she asked, groping for common sense.

'No problem. It's yours—remains yours. Our legal department will set up the contract.'

He whisked her away in a taxi, took her to the sort of restaurant she was familiar with from her modelling days and she realised with a shock that she was being seriously spoiled.

It must be true, then. They must be really excited about her work, or they would have taken her to the pub on the corner.

How strange. She tried to concentrate on the facts and figures, publishing schedules, printing and distribution, payment arrangements and so on, but she couldn't get past the projected royalties.

If she could do three of these little books a year, which they wanted her to, she could earn enough to support herself and the children. She could be independent, and not have to break her heart over Ben every time he was late home or went out unexpectedly.

He got the taxi to detour to the station, and dropped her off at Liverpool Street at three-thirty. She didn't get back to Ipswich station until five-fifteen, and by the time she arrived in Woodbridge it was nearly six.

The children would be frantic, she thought, and Ben would be coming home soon. She'd better pick them up straight away from Kate and hope she could get in before he did, because she hadn't worked out how to tell him yet.

In the old days it would have been wonderful. She would have rung him up and bubbled all over him, and he would have laughed with delight and taken her out for lunch and she would have told him all about it, and he would have looked at her contract and warned her of the pitfalls.

Now there was nothing between them but a cold and uncomfortable distance, and she felt sure this would make it even worse.

She abandoned the car on the drive and ran round to Kate's, and to her surprise the front door was ajar and she could hear raised voices. Puzzled, she went inside and then froze with horror. It was Ben, arguing with Kate, demanding to know where she was.

'I promised I wouldn't tell you, and I won't,' Kate was insisting firmly. 'She can tell you herself when she comes home.'

'She is coming home, then?' Ben asked, his voice like a whip.

'Of course she's coming home. Apart from anything else, she wouldn't leave the children, would she?'

He gave a harsh sigh. 'I don't know. I feel as if I don't know her any more. You're sure she hasn't gone to Oscar?'

Did she imagine it, or was there a thread of fear in his voice?

'Oscar?' Kate said incredulously. 'Why on earth would she go to Oscar? She hates him!'

'Are you sure? She used to love him.'

'Yes, I'm sure. She's got enough problems with you, without dragging Oscar back into the equation.' Kate broke off, and Liv heard something crash in the kitchen. 'Jake, put that down now. Go in the playroom. No, Ben, she hasn't gone to see Oscar, I'll tell you that much, although I don't see why you'd care. You're so indifferent to her—'

'Indifferent!' Ben exclaimed. 'Are you mad?'

'No, but she is, or getting that way. She thinks you regret it—marrying her. She's told me about your—arrangement.'

Liv closed her eyes. Oh, no, Kate, don't, she thought, but there was no stopping her friend now.

'What arrangement?' Ben said sharply.

'Your pseudo-marriage. Why did you do it, Ben? You could have just given her a place to stay. Why did you have to marry her, for heaven's sake?'

'Would you believe because I love her?' he said softly.

Liv felt the colour drain from her face. Even Kate was silent, but not for long.

'You love her? She doesn't think so. She thinks you're having an affair with your secretary.'

'Julie?' he said in astonishment. 'Why the hell would she think that?'

'Because you're never in? Because you don't show any interest in her except as a mother of your ready-made family? She's told me what you've said, Ben, how you yelled at her for trying to get her figure back—and do you know why she was doing it? Because she loves you, and you don't even notice her!'

'That's a lie,' Ben said softly. 'I do notice her. I can't get her out of my mind. That's why I keep going out—because I want a real marriage and she doesn't. She doesn't love me.'

'She wanted your baby.'

'Oh, yes—out of guilt, because she's got this crazy notion that she owes me. She's got this stupid independence thing—oh, hell—she hasn't gone on a photo-shoot, has she? For a catalogue or something?'

'No, I haven't,' Liv said, walking into the room behind him. 'I've been seeing a publisher—he wants me to write and illustrate children's books. So I can be independent, even though you think it's stupid.'

He looked at her, then back at Kate, and dragged a hand over his face. 'I think we need to talk,' he said roughly.

'I agree,' Kate said emphatically. 'I'll keep the kids, you go. I'll see you later—tomorrow, if necessary. Don't you dare come back until it's sorted out.'

He nodded at Kate, took Liv none too gently by the arm and wheeled her out. He didn't stop until they were at home, inside their own front door, and then he dropped her and stepped back.

'Is it true?' he asked, his voice harsh.

'Is what true? That I've been to a publisher? Of course it's true.'

'No. What Kate said—about you loving me.'

She looked at him—really looked at him, for the first time in ages, and saw pain etched deep in his eyes. Her shoulders dropped, and she nodded.

'Yes,' she said softly. 'It's true. I think I've always loved you, although I didn't realise it until you asked me to marry you.'

His eyes closed, and he swallowed convulsively and reached for her. 'Thank God,' he said unsteadily. 'I thought you'd left me. I thought you'd gone back to Oscar. I thought you hated me.'

'I don't hate you,' she said from the safety of his arms. 'I could never hate you. I just felt gutted, because you never noticed me. You couldn't watch me breastfeeding, you never wanted to touch me—'

'I thought you were still in love with Oscar!' he said, holding her away so he could look down at her. 'How could I tell you how I felt when you were on the rebound? It wasn't fair. I thought, if I married you, then maybe one day it would just all fall into place, but it seemed to get more and more difficult. And as for watching you breastfeeding, it turned me inside out just to see you. Do you have any idea how erotic it is for a man to see the woman he loves suckling a child?'

She took a deep breath, hardly daring to ask, but needing to know just the same.

'Do you love me?' she asked tightly, her insides in knots.

'I've always loved you,' he replied, his voice unsteady. 'Ever since you were fifteen years old and my mother took me on one side and threatened to castrate me if I laid a finger on you.'

She shook her head. It didn't add up. There was still the other woman—

'But you said you could never love again,' she protested. 'You said, ''Love like that happens only once in a lifetime, and it won't happen to me again.'' Was that when I was with Oscar? Is that when you met her?'

'Met who?'

'The woman you loved—the woman who broke your heart.'

He laughed softly, without humour. 'That was you, Liv. You broke my heart when you moved in with Oscar. I was getting ready to tell you that I loved you, and you told me instead that you were living with him.'

He took a steadying breath. 'I'd never realised it

could hurt so much,' he said quietly. 'I took myself off, swore off women and threw myself into work. And then you turned up on my doorstep with the children, like a parcel with a label on it saying "Delivered: one family", and I thought God had given me another chance with you, but you seemed so untouchable, so sad and vulnerable, and I didn't know what to do. It didn't seem like the right time to tell you that I love you.'

He gave a short laugh. 'That was when I hit on the bright idea of marrying you, and it all started to go wrong on our wedding night. I had to lie there next to you, wanting you to distraction and not daring to move in case you realised.'

'You should have covered me in chocolate body paint,' Liv said gently, reaching up to cup his cheek. 'I should have put on that nightie, and you should have put on that ridiculously small thong, and we should have taken advantage of all the satin and lace.'

He looked down at her and something happened in his eyes—something wonderful and tender and very, very sexy.

'It's not too late,' he murmured, and then added with endearing hesitation, 'Is it?'

She shook her head. 'No. No, Ben, it's not too late.'

'Good, because I have an overwhelming need to hold you, Liv, and touch you, and tell you how much I love you.'

He lifted her into his arms, making her feel tiny and feminine and delicate, and he carried her up the stairs and along to his room. The door was open. It was a good thing, Liv thought, because she had a feeling he wasn't letting anything stop him now and he would have simply kicked it out of the way!

He set her down on her feet, and stood back to look at her. 'You look very businesslike,' he said softly. 'We'll have to do something about that.'

He shed his jacket, then his tie, then reached for her, sliding the suit jacket down over her arms and off on to the floor. The skirt followed, shimmying down her legs and leaving electric shivers in its wake. 'Arms up,' he murmured, and peeled off the camisole, then stood back and looked at her.

'I'm feeling overdressed,' he said, and she smiled and reached for his buttons. They were small and fiddly, and her fingers were shaking, but she persevered, and finally they were all freed and he yanked the shirt out of his trousers and stripped it off. A cuff button flew across the room, and he grinned.

'Whoops,' he said. 'My wife will complain.'

'No, she won't,' Liv promised. 'I can guarantee it.'

She reached for the hook on his trousers, and he breathed in sharply as her fingers slid under the waistband. She eased them backwards and forwards, tormenting him, and finally his hands clamped on hers like iron and he eased them away. 'What are you trying to do to me?' he asked in a strangled voice.

'What I should have done weeks ago,' she said softly. 'I'm making love to you, Ben.'

He went still, and his hands came up and cupped her face, and he kissed her. It wasn't a clever kiss, not a skilful kiss using all the right moves—it was a kiss from the heart, the kiss of a man in need, the most powerful weapon in his armoury, and she went up on tiptoe and kissed him right back.

'I want you,' he said gruffly, lifting his head at last. 'I need you, Liv. I've been going crazy watching you for the last four months, and I don't think I can wait any more.'

'Good,' she whispered, and, sliding down his zip, she eased his trousers over his hips and let them fall. He toed off his shoes, kicked the trousers aside and pulled her back into his arms.

'Too far away,' he muttered.

'We could always lie down,' she suggested, and he lifted her and dropped her in the middle of the bed, following her down and lying full-length against her. Their legs tangled, their mouths found each other again and for a moment neither of them moved.

Then his hand came up, smoothing slowly over her hip, and he groaned. 'So soft,' he murmured. 'You're so soft—so smooth. You feel better even than in my fantasies.'

She ran her hand lightly over the broad sweep of his shoulder, feeling the warm satin of his skin overlying the bone and muscle and sinew beneath. So strong, so powerful, so male.

His hand cupped her breast through the lace of her bra. 'I want to touch you. I want to take everything off you and look at you—really look at you, instead of sneaking glances and catching glimpses and having to guess what you're like.'

'I'm a mother,' she reminded him, her confidence wavering, and he kissed her.

'I know. I know, and it makes you even more beautiful. Let me see you, Liv,' he murmured. 'Let me see all of you.'

So she lay there, her courage stretched to infinity, while his fingers fumbled with the catch on her bra. Then it was gone, and he slid it away and peeled her tights and little lacy knickers down her legs, leaving her naked and without anywhere to go.

'You are so lovely,' he whispered reverently, and he bent his head and took one breast in a hot, open-mouthed kiss that left her gasping. He moved his attention to the other, then his hand ran over the smooth curve of her abdomen and lingered on the soft nest of curls.

'I want you so much,' he said raggedly, lifting his head and staring down into her eyes. 'Please, Liv.'

His briefs did a very insignificant job of preserving his modesty, and she stripped them away in seconds, kneeling up beside him and running her hands over his long, well-muscled frame. His eyes glittered like sapphires, and he reached for her, drawing her down beside him.

'You wanted a baby,' he said roughly.

'Yes.'

'Good, because I don't have anything here to protect you from pregnancy.'

Her lips curved softly. 'Good. We'll take a chance. I need you—just you. Nothing between us. Just this time, at least, I want nothing between us.'

He rolled over her, pressing her down into the mattress, and he kissed her one more time. 'I love you, Liv,' he said tenderly, and then they were together, their bodies meshing in a wild dance that drove her over the brink of sanity and into a world she'd never even dreamed of. It fell apart around her, but he was there, holding her hard against his chest, sheltering her from the storm.

Then it reached him, too, and he stiffened and cried her name, and it sounded as if it had been dragged up from his very soul.

Then gradually the violence of their emotion retreated, leaving them locked in each other's arms, their hearts beating in unison.

'I love you,' she said again, and his arms tightened convulsively.

'I'm beginning to believe you. Perhaps a few more lessons like that and I'll be really sure.'

She smiled lazily. 'I'm sure it can be arranged. We've got all that chocolate body paint to use up—unless you threw it out?'

He coloured just a little. 'No, I didn't throw it out,' he admitted gruffly.

'It'll be awfully messy.'

'Perhaps later, in the bathroom?' he suggested, and she felt a chuckle rise in her chest.

'Sounds like fun.'

He laughed and hugged her, his body relaxed beside her now, and she rested her head on his shoulder and sighed contentedly.

'Tell me about this publisher,' he said out of the blue, and she could feel the tension enter his body again.

She lifted herself up on one elbow and looked down at him. 'I was doodling for Missy one day, and Kate saw me and said I ought to send some drawings in to a children's book publisher, so I did.'

He looked up at her, his eyes narrowed. 'And?'

She smiled. 'They loved them. They want to publish three a year, so I'm going to have to have somewhere to work—I thought the corner of the kitchen? Then I can watch the children. What do you think?'

'I'm stunned. I knew you wanted to do something, and I had a horrible feeling it was just to get away. I know things about the modelling industry that would make your hair curl, Liv—things that made me so sick when I found out that I wanted to kill. I was so scared for you, and when you talked about going back into it, I just felt sick.'

'David suggested porn,' she told him, and his arms tightened round her again.

'Don't,' he growled. 'Don't talk about him to me.'

She trailed her hand idly over his chest, threading her fingers through the light scatter of hair between his nipples. 'Do you mind about the books?' she asked carefully.

'Mind? No—of course I don't mind. Why should I mind?'

She shrugged. 'I don't know. You seem to have a thing about me being dependent on you—almost as if you need me relying on you for everything.'

'No,' he corrected. 'I don't need you to rely on me. I want you to feel you can, but I don't have a macho thing about supporting you or anything like that. And as for the books, I'm really thrilled for you. You've got so many talents, and I'm really glad they're being recognised. I'm proud of you, Liv. I've always been proud of you, and your children will be proud of you, too. You're an amazing woman, and I love you.'

His lips found hers, and with a sigh she gave herself up to him again.

It was much later when they went to collect the children from Kate. They had thrown on jeans and sweaters and run down the road like kids, and as Liv rang the bell she turned to Ben and smiled. 'Do you think we'll need to tell her?' she asked, but they didn't, of course.

Kate opened the door, took one look at them and

said, 'Thank God for that. Your children are asleep.
Leave them here for the night, they're fine.' She
paused and sniffed experimentally, then gave them a
quizzical look. 'Have you two been eating chocolates?'

NEARLYWEDS

Almost at the altar— will these *nearly*weds become *newly*weds?

Harlequin Romance® is delighted to invite you to some special weddings! Yet these are no ordinary weddings. Our beautiful brides and gorgeous grooms only *nearly* make it to the altar—before fate intervenes.

But the story doesn't end there....
Find out what happens in these tantalizingly emotional novels!

Authors to look out for include:

Leigh Michaels—The Bridal Swap
Liz Fielding—His Runaway Bride
Janelle Denison—The Wedding Secret
Renee Roszel—Finally a Groom
Caroline Anderson—The Impetuous Bride

Available wherever Harlequin books are sold.

HARLEQUIN®
Makes any time special ™

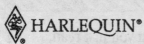

HARLEQUIN®

makes any time special—online...

eHARLEQUIN.com

your romantic escapes

—Indulgences—

♥ Monthly guides to indulging yourself,
such as:
★ Tub Time: A guide for bathing beauties
★ Magic Massages: A treat for tired feet

—Horoscopes—

♥ Find your daily Passionscope, weekly
Lovescopes and Erotiscopes

♥ Try our compatibility game

—Reel Love—

♥ Read all the latest romantic
movie reviews

—Royal Romance—

♥ Get the latest scoop on your favorite
royal romances

—Romantic Travel—

♥ For the most romantic destinations, hotels
and travel activities

If you enjoyed what you just read,
then we've got an offer you can't resist!

Take 2 bestselling love stories FREE!

Plus get a FREE surprise gift!

In March 2001,

Silhouette Desire

presents the next book in

DIANA PALMER's

enthralling *Soldiers of Fortune* trilogy:

THE WINTER SOLDIER

Cy Parks had a reputation around Jacobsville for his taciturn and solitary ways. But spirited Lisa Monroe wasn't put off by the mesmerizing mercenary, and drove him to distraction with her sweetly tantalizing kisses. Though he'd never admit it, Cy was getting mighty possessive of the enchanting woman who needed the type of safeguarding only he could provide. But who would protect the beguiling beauty from *him...?*

Soldiers of Fortune...prisoners of love.

Silhouette®
Where love comes alive™

Available only from
Silhouette Desire at
your favorite retail outlet.

Visit Silhouette at
www.eHarlequin.com

SDWS